snap decision (book one)

MAYBE TONIGHT?

snap decision
(book one)

MAYBE TONIGHT?

bridie clark

roaring
brook
press
new york

Dedicated to my children, godchildren, nieces, and nephews

Text copyright © 2013 by Bridie Clark
Published by Roaring Brook Press
Roaring Brook Press is a division of Holtzbrinck Publishing Holdings
Limited Partnership
175 Fifth Avenue, New York, New York 10010
macteenbooks.com

Library of Congress Cataloging-in-Publication Data
Clark, Bridie.
    Maybe tonight? / Bridie Clark.
        p. cm.
    Summary: "Invites the reader to participate in the high-stakes social
scene of Kings Academy, an elite boarding school where fitting in may
require selling one's soul"—Provided by publisher.
    ISBN 978-1-59643-816-3 (pbk.)
    ISBN 978-1-59643-818-7 (ebook)
    1. Plot-your-own stories.   [1. Interpersonal relations—Fiction.
2. Dating (Social customs)—Fiction.   3. Boarding schools—Fiction.
4. Schools—Fiction.   5. Plot-your-own stories.]   I. Title.

PZ7.C538May 2013
[Fic]—dc23

                                                    2012040908

Roaring Brook Press books may be purchased for business or promotional use. For
information on bulk purchases please contact Macmillan Corporate and Premium Sales
Department at (800) 221-7945 x5442 or by email at specialmarkets@macmillan.com.

First edition, 2013
Book design by Andrew Arnold
Printed in the United States of America

10 9 8 7 6 5 4 3 2 1

Vincit qui se vincit.
One conquers by conquering oneself.

snap decision (book one)

MAYBE TONIGHT?

PROLOGUE

Congratulations! Out of a pool of highly competitive candidates, you've been accepted into the freshman class at Kings Academy, thus joining a tradition of academic excellence that's produced more of our world's leaders (five presidents, at last count), thinkers (winners of Nobels, Pulitzers, Fulbrights . . . oh my!), doers (from Fortune 100 CEOs to Hollywood über-producers), and influencers (also known as the filthy rich) than any other boarding school in the world. It's the gateway to Harvard, Princeton, and Yale. Nobody in your family has ever gone to such an elite school, let alone on a full scholarship. Your freshman class is full of Somebodies, Future Somebodies, and Children of Somebodies.

Oh, and you.

But hey, like, no pressure.

As you'll soon learn, navigating a social life at Kings Academy can be even more harrowing than the academic workload, which would overwhelm Stephen Hawking. Every choice you make has consequences. Each decision determines who you're most likely to become. Your perfect ending may be out there, but only if you listen to your heart and follow it wisely.

Good luck. You're going to need it.

SNAPSHOT #1

Saturday, February 15, 8:15 p.m.
Pennyworth House

"You should always wear skirts," Annabel declares, fishing an adorable red and silver Marc Jacobs mini out of her closet and discreetly ripping off the price tag before tossing it at your head. You're sprawled across the bottom bed—hers—of your shared bunks, your head propped up against one of her monogrammed pillows. It smells faintly of rose oil, Annabel's signature scent. "Your legs are phenom," she says. "I would kill."

It's a struggle not to roll your eyes, since Annabel's legs are just short of a mile, but you don't doubt her sincerity. Annabel Lake always sees the best in everyone, especially you, her best friend since you met last September during Pre-Frosh week.

Was it really just *six months ago* that you first set foot on Kings' idyllic New Hampshire campus—even more breathtaking than in the brochures? It feels like a mini-lifetime. You and Annabel both had your heads buried in campus maps when you collided in front of the stern-looking statue of a former headmaster, over whose shoulders a student had draped a lacy pink bra.

"I'm such a klutz!" Annabel had been quick to apologize, as though the crash was her fault alone. She had the kind of beauty that was startling in its rarity. Flawless skin, dark hair, eyes the color of blue-green sea glass. She wore a weathered oxford shirt, jogging shorts, a Cartier tank watch, and a Nantucket tan. (As you'd soon discover, everything looked fabulous when Annabel was the one wearing it. Like when *Teen Vogue* suggested cinching an oversize Hanes T-shirt with woven garden twine then pairing with acid-washed jeggings and a fedora? On Annabel, the look was fresh and quirky. On you, it was "security lapse in the psych ward.")

"Are you okay?" she'd asked, reaching out a hand to steady you.

You'd stared up at her (see: mile-long legs) and felt insecurities you didn't even know you had rush to the surface. *This was a mistake. I* so *do not belong here. Mommmmy!*

But Mommy was still stuck in traffic back in the upper school parking lot, all your earthly belongings piled in the back of her beat-up Town & Country. Not that there was anything she could do, anyway. The decision to apply to Kings Academy had been yours and yours alone. You couldn't run to your parents after twenty minutes on campus because you felt intimidated.

After a deep breath, you asked Annabel if she had any clue where Pennyworth was, and she broke into a warm smile, thus revealing her one and only detectable flaw: slightly overlapped front teeth!

Oh, please. Her smile is *adorably* crooked and you know it.

It turned out Annabel was looking for the same dorm. After some more searching, together you found the majestic neo-Georgian manse (um, how could you have missed it?) tucked in a corner of the wide, grassy area known as the Quad.

Only then did you realize you and Annabel were both assigned to suite 304. Roommates.

Once you'd managed to get over the crippling sense of inadequacy that someone as—well, *perfect* was really the only word—as Annabel could trigger, you'd realized just how lucky you were. Annabel was a one-in-a-million friend. No wonder Henry Dearborn had immediately fallen for her.

Henry.

Ahem. Let's get back to the party prep, shall we? This is Midwinter's Night Dream, after all, the most important party of the year, and it's imperative that you look amazing, slash, not spend your time secretly pining over Henry, your best friend's boyfriend—a habit that's unproductive at best, self-destructive at worst.

"You're sure you don't mind me borrowing this?" you ask Annabel. You slide her skirt over your hips and zip, turning around in the mirror to see it from all angles. Looks pretty decent, you have to admit. Better than anything you have in your closet by a long shot.

"Don't be silly. You *have* to wear it."

It's the same exchange you have every time Annabel dips into her wardrobe to find you something to wear. Oh, yeah . . .

add super generous to her list of sterling qualities. If you've gained a modicum of social acceptance at Kings, you have Annabel to thank. You think back to Homecoming tailgate, the first real social event of the year, and shudder at the memory of what you'd planned to wear: a shapeless L.L.Bean sweater, slightly baggy Gap jeans, and running sneakers. Running sneakers, people! It was Annabel who'd diplomatically explained that even though the tailgate was held in a *parking lot,* you'd probably feel more comfortable in her dark wash Seven jeans and perfectly cut Italian suede jacket.

Sometimes you barely recognize yourself. It's crazy to think that just last year you were living in Hope Falls with your parents, trudging through your days at the local middle school—which was rustic, tiny, woefully underfunded—and privately lamenting the fact that you seemed to be grasping algebra faster than the algebra teacher. Ever since you could remember, you'd wanted more out of life—or at least, out of school—than your classmates, who seemed contentedly on track to marry and stay put in Hope Falls, much like your own parents had.

Then one day at the public library (your second home), you'd skimmed the author bio of a debut novel you'd enjoyed. The writer had graduated from Kings Academy, it said—and on a whim, you Googled the school. With a few short keystrokes, everything in your life began to change. The Web site, with its exhilarating descriptions of classes and extracurricular activities and events on campus, was like a portal into heaven. Before you knew it, you'd downloaded an application—and several weeks later, mailed it in. You'd even managed to take the requisite test, lying to your parents about why you wanted to spend a day alone in Providence. Their complete trust in you only made you feel worse about your dishonesty, and yet you couldn't bring yourself to give up this sudden but very powerful dream. You had to try.

For weeks you'd guarded the mailbox. When that white packet with the Kings insignia on the front finally came, you'd seized upon it like a wild dog, ripping out the letter inside, eyes feverishly scanning but not able to properly read—until you saw the word *Congratulations*. Congratulations! It was, bar none, the happiest moment of your life. But then, of course, you'd panicked over how to tell your parents. Would they feel like you were rejecting them somehow, by fleeing the hometown neither of them had ever left? Would they let you go?

They'd nearly burst with pride.

The next day, your father happily reported that he'd been able to work out the details of your scholarship with Kings' financial aid director. The day after that, your mother came home from her job at the grocery store with KINGS ACADEMY sweatshirts for all three of you, plus a bumper sticker for the car and a new collection of coffee mugs. She'd asked her manager for the morning off and driven nearly two hours to raid the campus store. Neither she nor your father shed a single tear when they dropped you off. Pride, excitement, amazement at the opportunity you'd managed to find for yourself—these emotions dominated the loss they must have felt dropping their only child, age fourteen, off at boarding school. They were nothing short of amazing and supportive.

"Now for shoes," Annabel says, breaking your thoughts. "I think we have to be practical. I mean, we are going to be tromping through the woods tonight. How about these?" She holds up a pair of knee-high black boots, made out of the most luxurious leather. "I think they'll be perfect!"

There are no bounds to her generosity. Sometimes you have to draw them yourself. "Thanks, Annabel, but I'll wear my own. I'd feel awful if those got trashed!"

There's been one weird catch to having a personal stylist as a roommate. Over the past few months, you've occasionally gotten the vibe that only Annabel understands that you're a scholarship student from a town so small that the Mobil gas station constitutes the Friday night hot spot for local teenagers. Your other friends seem to be under the impression that you're one of them; that you, too, were born to a world of wealth and privilege. For whatever reason—call it pride—you haven't gone out of your way to clarify.

The door slams open. Spider Harris and Libby Monroe, your other roommates, spill into your spacious bedroom with stolen dining hall glasses and a dusty bottle of Patron. "Pregame!" Spider cheers, setting up bar on Annabel's mahogany desk.

"You girls look gorgeous!" Libby gushes, pulling her

beautiful strawberry blond hair out of its ponytail and letting it cascade around her shoulders. Her hair is worthy of a shampoo commercial. She heads for Annabel's iPod dock and starts fiddling around until she finds some Rihanna to crank.

"Could you at least move my history paper, Spider?" Annabel protests. "I don't think it'll help my grade if it smells like Spring Break Cancun."

Libby snorts. She's dressed in her signature ultra-prep look: a slim-fitting pink cashmere sweater that shows off her lithe frame, a tiered corduroy skirt, and equestrienne boots. "Like Worth would ever give you less than an A," she says.

"Gag," Annabel replies.

Martin Worth: twenty-nine-year-old American history teacher with a zealous following of students (male and female) who think the guy walks on water. Yes, Worth looks like Taylor Lautner might in a decade, and yes, he's actually an engaging, thought-provoking teacher—but you've been immune to his charms ever since Annabel confided that Worth had told her he "couldn't stop thinking about her" when she went in with questions about the midterm. Gross. She shut him down, of course, but rumor has it that Worth makes that line work with a new girl each year.

"I heard he's been hooking up with Oona," Spider pipes in.

As the star goalie for the varsity soccer team, Spider takes pride in her dreadful nickname. She's cute, spunky, funny, and loyal as hell—one of your dearest friends. (Because she was so heavily recruited for sports, a big chunk of Spider's tuition is covered. She just has to keep her GPA up.) You've always adored her, ever since she charged into suite 304 right behind you and Annabel and dropped her duffel bags, overflowing with sports equipment and just a few items of civilian clothing, onto the common room floor. Spider's pure tomboy and hasn't seemed to notice that there are boys—and more than a few hot ones—at Kings. You and Annabel have privately discussed your hunch that Spider might be more into girls, but not yet ready to come out. Who knows?

"So who do we think will be there tonight?" asks Libby, grabbing the first shot Spider pours and throwing it back. She scrunches up her freckled nose and sticks out her tongue like it's medicine she's been forced to take. "Finally, a party. Doesn't it seem like it's been forever?"

"It's been a few weeks, Lib." You have to laugh. Libby's definitely the social butterfly of the group—a tendency she's inherited from her parents, who split their time between the Manhattan and Palm Beach social circuits. Libby was the one who heard about tonight's party in the first place. She came home from biology lab with a map of the Lakeshore Woods, handwritten in purple pen, showing exactly how to find where the seniors would set up the bonfire. "So yeah, to you, I guess that's like forever."

"Henry's going—right, Annie?" asks Libby.

Weirdly, it drives you crazy when Libby calls Annabel that. *Annie.* Maybe it reminds you that Annabel and Libby have known each other forever—or at least their families have. You were lucky to get into Kings, double lucky to get that scholarship, whereas Annabel and Libby have a long lineage at the school and it was a given that they'd be accepted. Just like it's pretty much a given that they'll graduate, no matter how many rules they bend or break. You eye the tequila. Headmaster Fredericks has a different standard for kids whose families can donate buildings or baseball fields. There's probably also a separate standard for soccer goalies who can defeat Exeter for the next four years straight. But if *you* get caught, you're out. It's that straightforward. In the immortal words of Beyoncé, don't you ever get to thinking you're irreplaceable.

"Henry will be there," Annabel assures Libby.

You try to ignore the fact that your heart skips a beat when she says this. Henry Dearborn is in a different league than any guy you've ever met before. A junior on deck to be *The Griffin*'s next editor-in-chief, he's recently been assigned to edit your articles for the school's award-winning newspaper. Between the newsroom and your dorm room, it's become impossible to avoid those penetrating gray eyes, that sexy smile, those unruly curls . . . and even when he's not there, it's a struggle to keep him out of your thought stream. The other morning you saw him walking through the Quad, textbook tucked under one arm, just the right amount of swagger—and it was like someone had piped in a schmaltzy love song and the world was moving in slo-mo.

Yep. It's that bad. Full-blown crush territory on the one guy you should definitely *not* be noticing that way.

"What about Oona? Think she'll go?" Spider asks. Clearly she's praying the answer is no. Oona de Campos is a manipulative, calculating bully as far as you're concerned—but Spider hates her even more. You've asked Spider what went down, but your friend is uncharacteristically tight-lipped with the details. There's a story there, for sure.

"She'll be there," says Libby, suddenly busy with the clasp of her clutch. You all try to overlook the fact that Libby chugs Oona's Kool-Aid. That's just Libby. Oona's the reigning Queen Bee-otch at Kings, and well, Libby can be a bit of a cool-chaser. Oona goes clubbing in Boston on the weekends and gets chauffeured back to campus by older guys in Porsches. On Parents' Weekend, rumor has it that her dad brought her E. Her mom floats around Europe and is remarried to Oona's dad's younger brother. And that's just the beginning. You almost can't fault the girl for being so horrendous.

Libby suddenly slaps her forehead. "I almost forgot! The Midwinter's Night Dream Curse!" She sprints out of the room.

"The *what*?" you ask. Spider and Annabel don't react much to Libby's outburst. You seem to be alone in having no clue what she's talking about.

"It's this old campus legend," Annabel explains.

"Freshman girls who go to the Midwinter's party are supposed to make a sacrifice," says Spider, taking another shot of Patron. She winces hard. "A senior on the team told me why, but I can't remember."

"The sacrifice is supposed to make her lucky in love," Annabel says. "It's probably a load of crap, but whatever."

"It's not crap," Libby says, returning to the room with her sky-blue eyes bulging as they do when she's extremely earnest. (Past bulge-worthy topics have included: The hotness of Billy Grover. The awesomeness of Gilt.com. The horror of you submitting yourself to a $15 haircut from the barber in town.) She's holding four small squares of thick ivory silk and her super-sharp needlepoint scissors.

"Why is it that the *guys* don't have to bleed for love?" Spider groans.

"Excellent question," you second.

"Please. You think there'll be freshman boys there? They're the lowest rung on the food chain, they're *so* not invited to Midwinter's." Without warning, Libby jabs the scissors into her own palm. You immediately slap both hands over your eyes. You'd be the world's worst vampire. In the past, the mere sight of blood has made you vomit, faint, or (on one cherished occasion involving your cousin William and a poorly positioned Slip 'N Slide) both. "Okay, Annie, you're up," you hear Libby say. Then it's Spider's turn. You sit on the edge of the bed, face still covered. *Just a few drops of blood.* There's nothing you'd love more than to find a great boyfriend. But is Libby's love curse for real . . . and is it worth the bloodshed?

You are most likely to . . .

→ *stick out your palm, cover your eyes, and hope you don't hit the floor. The last thing you need is a love curse on your hands. Continue to Snapshot #2 (page 15).*

or

→ *over Libby's protests, say you'd rather not. A self-inflicted wound is no way to get the party started. The curse can't be real, anyway. Continue to Snapshot #3 (page 20).*

SNAPSHOT #2

Saturday, February 15, 9:04 p.m.
Pennyworth House

The smell of moo-shu pork hangs in the air. You slowly crack your eyelids to find yourself in your dimly lit bedroom, stretched out on Annabel's lower bunk, her thick cashmere throw draped over your body. Your fingers find the inside of your left palm, sore and covered with a Band-Aid. Libby's BS curse. You'd gone last, dreading the moment when Libby would jab your hand with the needlepoint scissors. For good reason. A) It hurt like hell, and B) pretty much the nanosecond she did it, you'd felt your legs go boneless. Even now, the mere thought of that blood beading up in your palm makes you feel woozy.

"You fainted, sweetie," says Annabel gently. Sitting in the corner chair with the phone cradled to her cheek, she digs chopsticks into a white carton of Chinese takeout. "She just woke up, Caroline. I'd better jump. Sorry I made you late for your dinner." She pauses as her older sister, a sophomore at Harvard, says goodbye. "Love you, too."

Annabel crosses over to sit on the edge of her bed. "You

were kind of disoriented when you came to, so we let you fall back to sleep for a while. I called your parents, and they said to let you rest, that it's happened before when you see blood. How do you feel?"

Truthfully, not super. Your head is pounding a little, and you feel shaky.

"You want an ice pack?" She hands you one wrapped in a towel, and you press it gratefully against the back of your neck. "The nurse said it might help."

It does. Thank goodness you have Annabel to take care of you. She really is an amazing friend. "Did Libby and Spider go to the party? I'm sorry I grounded you, Annabel. I'm fine, seriously, if you want to take off—"

Your best friend shakes her head. "No way. You scared me. I already texted Henry, right after ordering our usual from Chow Fun. We'll all stay in, consume ungodly quantities of MSG, and watch *Friday Night Lights*." She claps her hands together in the universal gesture for "Don't fight me on this."

You sit up straight in bed, willing yourself to snap out of the fog. "I can't let you and Henry miss the party because of my lame fainting issue!" Unspoken thought bubble: the prospect of sharing a couch with the happy couple sounds so awkward, you'd rather pass out again. Where'd those scissors go?

"Henry doesn't mind. He offered to come over right away." Annabel smiles, but there's a distant look in her eyes that you pick up on instantly. "And I don't mind either. To tell you the truth, I didn't really feel like going in the first place. Henry and I had this weird talk last night. I think a night in is what we need."

"What do you mean, a weird talk?"

"Well, he kind of blurted that he might want to see other people." Annabel says this casually, picking lint off the back of the chair. "But I don't think he was serious. I was pestering him about his—*our*—plans for spring break. He backtracked right after he said it."

You try not to let your face reveal your shock. Their relationship has always seemed so blissful, it's hard to imagine that Henry could have so much as a flicker of doubt. "You guys should be alone then," you tell her.

"No need. We're fine, I promise. It was a blip." Annabel stands up and walks over to her dresser, where she runs a brush through her dark hair, which looks perfectly sexy against her leopard-print silk shirt. She reaches for a slip of white paper that's folded on the dresser and hands it to you. "By the way, Walter must've stopped by, but I guess in all the commotion of your fainting, nobody heard him knock. He left this."

M—

Stopped by at 8 o'clock to introduce you to my cousin, who's unexpectedly in town for the night. We're heading now to Glory Days Diner, if you'd like to come join us.

Yours,
Walter

You're not the least bit surprised that Walter Mathieson's not heading to the party. He's a freshman boy, and a nerdy one at that. You probably wouldn't have made the cut yourself—you just happen to be roommates with three girls who get asked to pretty much everything. But Walter might be the one kid in school who hasn't even *heard* about Midwinter's Night Dream. You and Walter are both on Student Council, which is how you met, and you became tight when you both were assigned to the anti-drug committee. You've spent the year brainstorming ways to raise campus awareness of the dangers of drug use, and Headmaster Fredericks himself has commended the work you've done. Even though you're both equally passionate about the mission, Walter tends to be more vocal about it. Frankly, it puts some of the cool crowd off. Although he's one of your closest pals, and one of the few people with whom you could truly be yourself, Walter is definitely on the outskirts of the Kings social scene—a fact that seems to bother you more than it does him.

"Why don't you tell Walter to come over?" Annabel flops down at the end of the bed. "Plenty of food to go around."

You are most likely to . . .

→ *convince Annabel that you're up for the party. It's been the headline for weeks . . . no way any of you are missing it. Continue to Snapshot #4 (page 23).*

or

→ *convince Annabel to cut you loose and head back to the party with Henry. You'll spend the night with Walter and his cuz. So what if it's not the big night you'd planned? Continue to Snapshot #5 (page 30).*

SNAPSHOT #3

Saturday, February 15, 8:21 p.m.
Pennyworth House

"**Don't come crying to me when you're sad and loveless,**" Libby teases you, although you know she's kind of serious. She tucks three silk squares—now dotted with blood like mini–Japanese flags—into the pocket of her skirt. "A few drops of blood, a lifetime of love. You're sure?"

"You take this stuff too seriously, Lib," Annabel says.

"I'm sure," you say, feeling anything but.

There's a knock at the door, a familiar *rat-a-tat-tat*, and Libby's eyes flash with alarm. "Tell me you didn't invite Walter," she whispers.

Walter Mathieson may not be the coolest, but he's a totally solid friend and you love spending time with him. You can be yourself with Walter, you can dork out completely, and he'll never judge. Sure, sometimes you wish he would put in a little effort to fit in. For one thing, he wears the same exact outfit—the "Wal-iform" as you've come to think of it—every single day. Maroon sweater with gray stripes. Old chinos. White Converse All Stars. You're one of the few who know that Walter has five identical sets of this outfit in his closet. Everyone else, naturally, assumes he has a hygiene issue. You've tried to delicately explain—but Walter just says that he hates wasting time on clothes and it's easier this way. He carries a small canvas knapsack everywhere, like Linus with his security blanket. Inside are his necessities: a small chess set, some book of philosophy (right now he's obsessed with Sartre), a leather-bound journal, grape bubblegum, and a comb in a comb sheath. Yeah . . . a comb sheath. Besides being textbook nerdy, the comb is ironic, given the dimensions and general unruliness of Walter's mane of curls.

Rat-a-tat-tat.

"Maybe it's Tommy or Lila," whispers Spider. Tommy is short for Thomasina, but call her that and she'll have you deboned. Tommy and Lila are so-called honorary roommates, because they spend more time in your common room than their own. They both hail from Southern states and don't leave their room without curling their hair first. It's funny—for the amount of time you've spent in their presence, you don't yet feel like you know either girl all that well.

"Tommy's going with her lacrosse friends. Lila's got the stomach flu or something," reports Libby. Of course, she's got the up-to-the-minute scoop on everyone's plans. "Trust me. It's Walter."

She's probably right. Walter's probably overheard someone talking about the party and is hoping to walk over with you, just to take a look. Sometimes he takes an anthropological interest in the social behavior of his peers.

"Play dead," Libby tells you. You look to Spider and

Annabel but they avoid your eyes. Clearly they'd rather keep the pre-party to the four of you, too. They're always nice to Walter, but that doesn't mean they want to do shots with him on a Saturday night.

You are most likely to . . .

tell Libby to shove off and you answer the door, inviting Walter to join your group. Continue to Snapshot #6 (page 35).

or

make like a possum until Walter leaves. He probably wouldn't have fun, anyway. Continue to Snapshot #7 (page 39).

SNAPSHOT #4

Saturday, February 15, 9:28 p.m.
Lakeshore Woods

"Seriously, you're sure you're feeling up for this?" Henry asks again as the three of you hack your way through the woods en route to the party. He's looking more adorable than usual tonight in faded Levis and a heavy Irish fisherman's sweater, and he gallantly directs the flashlight so that you and Annabel can keep an eye on your footing. You crunch pine needles as you walk, releasing their delicious fragrance in the air.

Other than the tiny fact that Henry kissed Annabel on the cheek, not the lips, when he showed up at your room, there doesn't seem to be anything off between them—no visible signs of trouble in paradise. Annabel must be right. Henry's "seeing other people" comment was just a blip. They'll live happily ever after, no doubt. Which is good for your best friend, so happy up.

"Totally sure," you answer. "You guys can stop worrying about me." You smile gratefully at them. At least you're lucky to have them both as friends. They'd been willing to give up the biggest party of the year just to make sure you were okay. Now if you could only keep that in mind—and stop wondering what it would feel like to kiss Henry, to feel his hands on your hips, pulling you closer—

"Wow!" Annabel squeezes your hand as you reach the clearing. The sight is so spectacular your breath catches in your throat. The bonfire is mammoth, enveloping you immediately in delicious heat, and the seniors have cast a net of tiny white lanterns through the branches of the surrounding birch trees. The lanterns spill a dancing light over everyone, transforming a crowd of trust-fund kids drinking beer from plastic cups into frolicking wood nymphs and fairies at a bacchanal. It's beyond beautiful. You can't help but feel there's something enchanted about this night. That anything could happen if you let it.

From across the crowd, Libby spots you guys and hustles over. You recognize the pink flush in her cheeks and hope that she'll at least pace her drinking better than she usually does. "Feeling better?" she asks you, not bothering to wait for a response. "I already threw our sacrifice on the fire. Don't worry, sweetie, I managed to get some blood from you before you hit the floor. We're curse-free."

You pantomime wiping your brow with relief. But Libby's no longer looking at you. As usual, she's shifted her focus to Annabel, her idol. It must irk Libby that Annabel favors you over her.

As the two of them chat, you sneak up behind Spider,

who's waiting in line at the keg, and slap her butt, causing her to jump a mile. "Dude!" she grins when she sees it's you. She's the only girl at the party dressed appropriately for the February frost in her thick hoodie and windpants. "How are you? Sorry to abandon, but you know Libby had to get here"—eye roll—"and it seemed dangerous to let her navigate the woods on her own." Spider grew up on a horse farm in Kentucky and loves to tease Libby for her complete lack of "nature survival skills." Libby teases Spider right back about nonexistent manure under her fingernails and the fact that she calls jeans "dungarees." Despite their abundant differences, the two seem to have forged an unexpected bond. It gives you hope that there's more to Libby than meets the eye.

As the two of you inch closer to the keg master—an abrasive senior girl you recognize from school assemblies—you sense the presence of Crosby Wells behind you in line. You elbow Spider, who's busy imitating Libby on the hike but quickly clues in. Crosby Wells is a senior, and sexy in a scruffy, guitar-toting, thrift-store-shopping, long-haired lead singer kind of way. He's not for everyone, but Crosby does something for you. You've never had the chance (read: always been too chicken) to talk to him. Spider, of course, knows this.

She whips around. "Is your band going to play tonight?"

You feel blood rush to your cheeks. Leave it to Spider. No points for subtlety, but no demerits for shyness.

"Uh, no," says Crosby, tucking a piece of his dark hair behind his ear. "Our drummer's got a stomach thing." His skin is a perfect golden tan, meaning he's probably just returned from some sick getaway—a long weekend in Turks and Caicos, winter recess in Careyes. (The past six months have been Jetsetting 101. You can now talk the talk about powder conditions in Vail and Telluride, even though you've never actually been on skis.)

"Have you heard Crosby's band? They're pretty awesome," Spider asks you, drawing you into the conversation. The girl's a pro.

You force yourself to act cool and confident—or, at least, to form words. "I think I was home when you all went. What instrument do you play?" You fully know the answer, of course— who hasn't seen Crosby strumming his acoustic guitar all over campus?

"A little of everything and a lot of guitar," he says, seeming to notice you for the first time. When he smiles, you feel instantly more relaxed.

"Keep your cup!" the keg master barks at you as she hands you a foamy beer.

Crosby hands over his cup next. "If you're interested, my band is playing at the Spigot next weekend. We're hoping for a big crowd from Kings." It's just you and him now; Spider has discreetly slipped into a conversation with a player from the guys' soccer team who's standing farther back in the line.

"I would love that. I just don't know if I can get in."

"No ID?"

"No ID."

Crosby's brow furrows. "Easy enough fix. I'll ask my cousin. She looks a little like you." He pauses to drink his freshly re-filled beer. "She's, like, a model in Paris." He slips this in so nonchalantly that for a second you think you've heard him wrong. *Excusez-moi?* Did Crosby Wells just say you in any way resemble a *model in Paris?* On top of which, did he offer to go out of his way to score you a fake ID?

The next thing you know, Crosby's guiding you through the flickering light toward a felled tree, where a bunch of his buddies—the cool, artsy crowd that favors dreadlocks and multiple piercings, "nonconformists" who seem to "noncon-form" in the same ways—are hanging out. "Nico, don't you think she could pass with Colette's ID?" he asks a guy roll-ing a cigarette. Nico looks you up and down for a second and shrugs.

"Nico plays bass in Cosmic Cowboy," Crosby tells you.

"Cosmic Cowboy?"

"Our band."

"Oh. Cool." Cosmic Cowboy? Well, naming a band must be hard. And lots of great bands have names that sound pretty random before you hear their music. Wedding Present? Ma-roon 5? Red Hot Chili Peppers? The Beatles? Cosmic Cow-boy isn't much worse.

While Crosby's telling you about his favorite bands, you rack your brain for some cool choices of your own to wow him with should there be a moment to speak. You love music almost as much as you adore books—and yet it's always a struggle to answer questions like "If you could choose three albums to be stranded with on a deserted island, what would they be?" or "Who's your favorite author?"

Fortunately he doesn't ask those questions, or any. Instead, Crosby takes your hand in his. You can feel the calluses on his fingertips. Oddly sexy, although you're a little stunned by how quickly he's coming on to you. Maybe your luck with guys really has changed. In any case, the night seems to be unfolding in unexpected and decidedly thrilling ways.

As the two of you sit on the knocked-over tree, your bodies close, you notice the light from the bonfire dims—and look up to find Henry standing five feet away. He doesn't say anything, but seems to be glowering at you and Crosby.

"Henry, hey! Um, do you know Crosby?" you ask, but Henry doesn't answer. Whoa. What's with the awkward showdown feeling? And why does Henry's stance suggest that he might like to take a Tyson-size bite out of Crosby's ear?

"We've met," he says tersely, looking only at you. "How are you feeling? Probably not the best idea to be drinking." He glances at Crosby. "She passed out earlier."

Why is Henry acting like a protective—make that crazily overprotective—big brother? Your eyes cast around for Annabel, who might be able to explain. You quickly spot her, not far from Henry—motionless, watching the scene with wide eyes. Suddenly Annabel moves toward her boyfriend. Once she reaches him, she puts her hand on Henry's shoulder, never acknowledging you or Crosby, and whispers something in his ear.

Henry shakes his head at whatever she's saying, looking even more flustered. He and Annabel step away now but you can still hear them. "I just don't want to see your friend get taken advantage of," he says to her.

Henry is trying to protect you from Crosby? Why?

Annabel just looks at Henry one last time before she turns and runs toward the woods, disappearing down the path you'd emerged from not long ago.

You are most likely to . . .

dash after your BFF. Clearly Annabel's pretty distraught—she could use a friend. Continue to Snapshot #8 (page 42).

or

let Henry go after her. They seem to be in the middle of something—better to let them work it out. And you'll get to see what happens next with Crosby. Continue to Snapshot #9 (page 47).

SNAPSHOT #5

Saturday, February 15, 9:15 p.m.
Glory Days Diner

You know that moment at the end of a super-long day when you slip your aching feet out of your boots and skinny jeans (the ones that are a little too snug in the waist but you keep wearing them anyway), shed your bra, lose the scratchy sweater, and slip into those fuzzy blue pajamas from the bottom of your drawer? Walter is the human embodiment of that moment.

Glory Days is pretty much empty tonight, other than a few locals hanging at the counter. As soon as you swing open the door, you spot Walter in your regular booth, talking animatedly between sips of Cherry Coke (his favorite), and feel instantly glad you decided to join him. Mom always says the mark of a true friend is simply that you're happier in his or her presence, and that's the case with Walter. You can talk about anything with him—the meaning of an e.e. cummings poem, the best road food between school and Boston (an ongoing debate), and even intimate family stuff that you wouldn't feel comfortable sharing with Annabel. You met when you were both elected class representatives to the Student Council—not exactly highly sought-after positions, you were the only two freshmen to run—and you got to know each other well through your work on the anti-drug committee.

"You made it!" he grins, giving you a big squeeze as soon as you slide into the red pleather booth next to him. As usual, he's wearing his "Wal-iform"—maroon-and-gray sweater, old chinos, and the canvas knapsack he's never seen without. Annabel once put it perfectly when she said that Walter dresses the way her father *would* if left to his own devices. "This is my cousin Helen."

You look across the table, hand already extended, and then the world seems to grind to a screeching stop.

Helen?

Helen, the cousin who caught bullfrogs with Walter during summers up in Maine? Helen, the cousin who helped Walter build his first model rocket? Your mind is reeling. Because Helen is not Helen. Helen is . . . HUNTER MATHIESON. *The* Hunter Mathieson. How had it escaped your attention that Walter's cousin was a megastar? The one starring in that new chick flick with Ashton Kutcher. The one rumored to have broken up Justin Timberlake and Jessica Biel. The one who caught flak for that *Vanity Fair* cover (which, for the record, you found perfectly tasteful and artistic, even before you knew she was Walter's cousin). Meanwhile, seconds are ticking by. Come back to earth! Don't just gape like a weirdo—say something! But you can't seem to form words. It's hard to speak when your jaw is on the floor.

"I kind of forget that you're famous now," you hear Walter chuckle.

"I'm so glad to meet you," Hunter says, extending her hand across the table. She speaks quietly, as though afraid of drawing attention, but her voice sounds unmistakably like it does in movies—warm, rich, the same honey-coated Midwestern twang as Walter. Now that you know to look for it, you can see the family resemblance. It makes you notice for the first time how great Walter's bone structure is . . . and he's got those baby blue eyes, too. You watch her tap the contents of a Sweet'N Low packet into her coffee. This is insane. Your second out-of-body experience in one night. "Walter's told me a lot about you, but he didn't tell me you were so pretty," Hunter says, all charm. Poor Walter turns five shades of red.

Thankfully, his embarrassment snaps you out of your celebrity stupor. You manage to regain some composure and ask Hunter if she's just in town for the night or a longer visit.

Hunter fiddles with one of the five diamond studs in her left earlobe; her right earlobe is bare. "I'm supposed to be in New York, at this premiere thingy, but I decided to play hooky and told the pilot to swing up here instead. My agent is going to be pissed, but whatever. I just needed to see Walter and regroup for, like, a second. My life has gotten so overprogrammed." She's talking quickly, like she's had four cups of coffee leading up to this one. You notice some spinach from her salad has lodged next to her bicuspid. She's just a person—albeit one with her own private plane and "premiere thingies" in New York City to attend. Your heart rate is slowly returning to normal.

Walter shakes his head in frustration. "You've always been so independent. Maybe you need to take back some control from your team."

"Easier said than done." Hunter picks up a greasy fry from his plate, studies it carefully from every angle, and allows the tip between her pink lips. She takes a minuscule bite and puts the rest down on her plate. "Anyway, I shouldn't complain. It's just nice to be here and have a minute of my own time." No sooner have the words left her mouth than her phone starts rattling the gold-flecked linoleum table. She peers at the screen with one eye and then scowls. "What'd I tell you? My agent."

"Would you like me to answer it?" Walter offers. "Tell him you're not available?"

Hunter smiles fondly at him. "Thanks, but no. I'm being childish." She picks up the phone and immediately you hear a man barking at her through the tiny holes. Next to you, Walter stiffens, protective of his cousin. "Jake, I'm sorry. I know. I'm sorry. I know," she says quietly, slumping on her side of the booth as she takes a verbal spanking from her agent. She looks so small and defeated—it makes you want to jump to her defense, too. "I can't make it to New York tonight after all. I'm with friends right now." Walter gives her thumbs-up for standing her ground. "Scorcese will be there? I didn't know that." Her agent yells some more words at her. "I didn't know," she interjects. More shouting. "Two. Maybe. Let me ask. I'll call you back in three seconds." She hangs up and puts down the phone. You're surprised it's not steaming. That guy has some serious anger management issues.

"Okay, guys." From the other side of the booth, Hunter Mathieson seems to instantly forget her agent's abusiveness. She unleashes the megawatt smile that won America's hearts. "How would you like to come with me to New York for a little party?"

You are most likely to . . .

→ *sneak out and party it up! Even though you could get expelled for leaving campus without written permission from your parents or a faculty adviser, how can you pass up the chance to party in New York with A-list celebs? Continue to Snapshot #10 (page 50).*

or

→ *turn down the invite. As fabulous as it sounds . . . you're toast if you get caught, and it doesn't seem worth the risk. After all, it's nothing less than your entire future at stake. Do you really want to go back to Friday nights at the Mobil station and a calculus teacher who dozes off in class? Continue to Snapshot #11 (page 54).*

SNAPSHOT #6

Saturday, February 15, 8:22 p.m.
Pennyworth House

You open the door to find Walter with his knapsack, standing next to a petite redhead who looks an awful lot like . . . but it can't be . . . Hunter Mathieson?!? Hunter Mathieson is standing in your hallway. Smiling at you. Like a normal person, which of course she's *not*, since normal people don't get aerially photographed lounging on Jay-Z's yacht in St.-Tropez. The wide-set blue eyes, the chiseled cheekbones you've seen on the big and small screen dozens of times—the gleaming smile you've seen stretched across billboards—the body you've seen scantily clad on the cover of *Vanity Fair*—is now standing three feet away, with her arm linked through Walter's!

"Good, you're home," he says, beaming. "I wanted you to meet my cousin Helen." He turns to his cousin. "Or I guess it's Hunter now—but you'll always be Helen to me. Anyway, she surprised me by flying in for the night."

"Helen?" You sound like an idiot, but you can't contain your shock. Walter had mentioned having a cousin named Helen, also an only child, with whom he used to go on camping trips during the summer. Helen had once smuggled a bullfrog home and hid it from her parents for over a month, until it escaped . . . only to resurface during her mother's bubble bath. You dimly recall Walter gushing about Helen's ability as an actress, but he'd never mentioned that she was *Hunter Mathieson*! Before you can pull yourself together, your roommates crowd around you at the door. Libby's eyes may just pop straight out of her head. The girls all eagerly shake Hunter's hand and Libby yanks her and Walter into the suite.

"This is *so* not what I expected a dorm room to look like," says Hunter, nodding appreciatively at the decor. Immediately after move-in, Libby's mother had flown in her interior decorator—a pinch-faced Park Avenue type who claimed your neon beanbag chair would haunt her dreams—to "redefine the space." In no time, your standard issue dorm room had been swathed in pale lavender and cream with ikat-covered couches, high-gloss end tables, and a beautiful needlepoint carpet. Fresh peonies were delivered every Thursday. Just like home, you know?

"We wanted to make it our own," says Libby, waving her hand in the air with a flourish you imagine she inherited from her mother. Spider rolls her eyes. "*Elle Décor* totally wanted to run a piece, but the school said no." Libby guides Hunter toward the bedroom she shares with Spider, an explosion of tangerine and hot pink. From the sculptural chandelier to the crisply ironed bedding (courtesy of a biweekly cleaning service), the room screams Libby and makes Spider want to scream. "Walter, you guys *must* come to the Midwinter's party tonight," Libby says, laying her hand on his shoulder as though they're old chums. "It's going to be epic. Some seniors throw it every year. There'll be a huge bonfire—"

This from the girl who was just begging you not to open the door for him?

"That's nice of you, but Helen just got in from L.A." Walter looks over at his cousin to gauge her enthusiasm. "She may just want to grab dinner and take it easy."

Libby gapes at him in disbelief. Epic? Seniors? *Bonfire?* What didn't he get?

"I'm game for anything, Wal," says Hunter, smiling at him as she crosses the room to sit on a couch. She loosens the burnt-orange cashmere scarf she's draped several times around her neck. "A party in the woods? Maybe we can even hunt for a bullfrog or two."

Libby's grin reaches a wattage that could power an entire village in Guatemala. "Yay!" she shouts, clapping her hands together and spontaneously kissing Walter on the cheek.

She'll never try to exclude him again, you think, feeling a tremendous sense of relief. Being related to Hunter Mathieson equals instant and irrevocable cool points. Spider doles out two more shots. She hands you a chipped mug that reads I RUN LIKE A GIRL . . . TRY TO KEEP UP. You stare at the clear brown liquid, swish it around under your nose. Smells like it could strip paint.

"Bottoms up!" says Annabel, clinking her glass with the rest of the group.

You are most likely to . . .

throw back a shot, feeling it burn its way down your throat. Continue to Snapshot #12 (page 58).

or

mutter some excuse about a tequila allergy before passing your shot off to Libby, who's always happy for more. Continue to Snapshot #13 (page 64).

SNAPSHOT #7

With each passing second of silence, you feel like more of a cowardly jerk. You feel awful for ignoring Walter's knock. He would never do that to you. Then again, he probably would've hated the party. Walter is happiest with his nose buried in a book. He'd spend the evening in peaceful solitude, reading and listening to Brahms, instead of trekking through the cold, dark woods to get to a glorified keg party. His only real reason for going would be to hang with you.

If you'd been trying to reassure yourself, you failed: the thought that Walter wants nothing more than your company pricks at your conscience even more.

"I think he's gone," says Libby, tiptoeing to the doorway. You feel a surge of animosity toward her. It's just lame how much stock she puts in who's cool and who's not. Sometimes you wonder whether you and Libby would be friends at all had you not been randomly assigned to live together. If Annabel hadn't given you her seal of approval, would Libby have decided you didn't make the cut, either? Would you have been shunned like Walter? Libby returns to the bedroom with a small piece of white paper, folded, and hands it to you. "He slipped this note underneath the door."

You open it and read:

M—

Stopped by at 8 o'clock to introduce you to my cousin, who's unexpectedly in town for the night. We're heading now to Glory Days Diner, if you'd like to come join us.

Yours,
Walter

Yours. Did he have to write that?

Spider hands you a shot, glancing at the note. "So he had plans already. It's not like he's sitting home alone." She's trying to make you feel better, but it doesn't work. She passes out the other shots. You take a sniff of the tequila and your head automatically rears back a little, repulsed by the toxic smell. Yuck. Your mind drifts to the cheese fries and chocolate milk shakes at Glory Days. And back to Walter. What if he knew you were really behind the door, waiting for him to leave? It's a devastating thought.

"Bottoms up, ladies!" says Annabel.

You are most likely to . . .

take a shot. Maybe it'll help you forget what a jerk you were to your pal. The tequila sears your throat. Continue to Snapshot #14 (page 69).

or

pass. You've already caved to peer pressure once tonight, and it made you feel pretty miserable. It feels better to say no this time. Continue to Snapshot #15 (page 73).

SNAPSHOT #8

Saturday, February 15, 10:18 p.m.
Lakeshore Woods

"Annabel! Will you please wait!" You've been chasing her through the woods, but the distance separating you seems to only grow. It doesn't help that Annabel's got four inches on you and runs like a gazelle. "I'm feeling light-headed again!"

Okay, that was cheap. But you can hear her footsteps slow, and then stop. Finally. Moments later you reach her.

"What happened? Are you okay?" you pant.

Her back is toward you and she doesn't turn around when you approach. She just shakes her head, her raven hair so lustrous it reflects the moonlight. "It's Henry. I think it's over."

"That's impossible!" It instantly feels like a stupid thing to say, but you mean it. Henry and Annabel are the gold standard of coupledom. They've always seemed so in love, so compatible, so happy.

"First he says we should consider seeing other people—"

Annabel's crying now—crying hard. Her words come out in the staccato of a child who's been hurt and can't catch her breath through her tears. Your heart is breaking next to hers.

What is Henry's problem? Has he not noticed that his girl-friend is absolutely and utterly perfect? Your loyalty to Annabel flares up in anger toward him, overriding your crush. How could he hurt her like this?

"I hoped I could talk him out of it. But then tonight"—another hiccuping sob escapes Annabel's lips—"watching how jealous he got when you were talking to Crosby, I knew. I knew it was over. And I knew why."

She can't be saying what she's saying. Both your hands fly to your cheeks in complete and utter shock. It isn't possible that—

"I think Henry is in love with you!" Annabel's face seems to crumble in her pain. "It's like some horrible Jerry Springer episode! My boyfriend secretly lusts after my best friend! How can this be happening?"

She's practically hyperventilating, and you're not far behind her. "That can't be true, Annabel. Henry and I are only friends through you, and he was just worried about me because of the whole fainting thing!" But even as the words leave your lips, you can see that there might be more to it than that. Henry had looked ready to sock Crosby in the face. He'd rushed to your room when he heard you'd fainted and had been genuinely concerned about your decision to head to the party. Not to mention that recently all of your articles for *The Griffin* had been assigned to Henry for editing. It had struck you as an unlucky coincidence—more time together, more unwanted fuel for your crush. But could he have been pulling strings to work with you?

Annabel wipes her tear-streaked cheek with the back of her hand. "It's more than that. He always wants to talk about you. He actually *quoted* from that poem you wrote for the lit magazine. He's weirdly curious about your reactions to things, your plans . . . Just trust me. I'm not an idiot."

A secret, dangerous feeling has taken root inside you. Even though it's wrongity wrong wrong, even though it makes you feel like the vilest person and worst friend on the planet, you can't deny that a small part of you hopes that Annabel's right.

"Let's get you home." You wrap your arm around her waist to support her, as though she's got a sprained ankle and not a broken heart, and the two of you begin to walk. The wild fury that had sent your best friend sprinting through the woods is gone now, and Annabel's footsteps have become heavy, as though gravity is doubling down on her.

"How can he do this?" she asks. Her voice trembles.

"I have no idea. You are amazing. You are the most incredible girl I know." It's true. You wish you had the right words to tell Annabel just how much you love her, how highly you regard her. "Maybe this is just a misunderstanding. You guys need to talk. You'll work it out."

She stops trudging and looks at you. The light from the moon is just bright enough for you to see her eyes. "Promise me you'll never be with him," she pleads, like she's been reading your guiltiest thoughts.

"Come on, that's crazy." You pull on her elbow, but she stays rooted in place. You want to yank her arm and force her to walk, but you don't.

"Will you please promise me?"

In the distance, you can hear a howl of laughter from the party. It sounds much louder than it did an hour ago, when you were making your way here with Annabel and Henry—the mirth slowly spreading its way through the New Hampshire forest, the party taking over the night. The two of you are alone in your unhappiness and confusion.

"You're going to have every guy at Kings in a line down our hallway, you know that?" you answer, evading the question. Your thoughts are reeling. It seems far-fetched that Henry would choose you over perfect Annabel—but the part of you that has always felt stuck in her shadow relishes the thought. And then there's the idea that you and Henry could actually be together. You can't think of anything you want more than that, more than him.

But if it means devastating your best friend? You reach for Annabel's hand. She is the most generous, sweet, caring friend imaginable. You love her. She's given you so much, and never asked anything in return.

Promise me you'll never be with him.

Never?

And now she's asking so much.

You are most likely to . . .

→ promise that Henry's off-limits. Your best friend is devastated. Like Annabel, you'll just have to find some way to move on. Continue to Snapshot #16 (page 78).

or

→ resist making a promise you don't want to keep. You love Annabel, but is it fair of her to ask you to sacrifice your own happiness for hers? Continue to Snapshot #17 (page 82).

SNAPSHOT #9

"Whoa. That was heavy." Crosby reclaims your hand as the two of you watch Henry dash after Annabel, but you barely notice now. From across the crowd, you catch Libby's eye. Billy Grover's arm is draped over her shoulder. The confused expression on her face tells you she's witnessed the strange scene between Annabel and Henry. She cocks her head as if asking a question, and you shrug. You don't know any more than she does.

Except maybe you do.

An outlandish thought has just flown into your head: maybe, just maybe, Henry has feelings for you, too. It would explain his reaction to seeing you flirt with Crosby—and if Annabel thought the same thing, that her boyfriend was into her BFF, it would explain her wigged-out dash into the creepy dark woods.

Could he? Your throat tightens at the thought.

"I think you'd really dig some of our newer stuff," Crosby says, his voice piercing through the fog of your thoughts. He's playing gently with your fingers. "If you wanted, we could head back to my room and I could play some of it for you."

Code for "let's go make out," obvi—and it snaps you back to the present. Could Crosby Wells—the hottie you've found too intimidating to talk to all year but have admired from afar—really be interested in you? As if answering your question, Crosby leans in and kisses you. He's a good kisser, in a way that suggests he's had plenty of practice, and you feel yourself getting pulled into the moment. It's your first real kiss, not counting a few dry pecks at summer camp. Crosby Wells—widely accepted as a Top Five senior stud—is making out with you. It happened so fast, and it's a bit surreal that it's happening at all.

"Should I not have done that?" he asks, grinning slyly as he pulls away. He's clearly a guy unused to the word *no*. You open your mouth but can't seem to think of an appropriate response. "So what do you say? Want to go check out some tunes?"

This is all moving at warp speed. Suddenly you're struck by the fact that Crosby doesn't even know your last name. Does he even know your first? Henry, you can't help but compare, knows you love fruity gum but a mere whiff of spearmint makes you want to chunder. He's met your parents and talked Red Sox stats with your dad. He knows how homesick you are for your golden retriever, Bernie, and how much you loved his predecessor Rufus, who was hit by a car when you were twelve. He's seen you with zit cream on your face, wearing your nightgown with Snoopy silk-screened on the front. He knows your passion for writing—how you'll stay in the newsroom until all hours of the night, struggling to get a piece locked down just right.

But what does it matter? He belongs to Annabel. Even if they break up, even if he does like you, he can never really be yours . . . unless you're willing to lose your best friend.

And here you are with gorgeous Crosby gently kissing your neck, looking for an answer.

You are most likely to . . .

go. Maybe Crosby can take your mind off Henry . . . it's worth a try. Continue to Snapshot #18 (page 91).

or

ask for a raincheck, knowing that Crosby will find another girl by the end of the night to take your place. You're admittedly a little nervous about going home with him and getting in over your head—and your heart is still stuck on Henry. Continue to Snapshot #19 (page 97).

SNAPSHOT #10

Saturday, February 15, 11:34 p.m.
New York City

"Hunter! Over here!" screams a photographer, throwing elbows at the rest of the pack outside Oberon (*the* nightclub right now, Hunter had explained mid-flight) to get his money shot. Hunter angles her body away from him and glances back provocatively, a total pro, rocking the pose you've seen so many times on the pages of *People* and *Us Weekly*. During the plane ride, she'd changed into a minuscule white minidress and some towering and wickedly sexy stilettos. Now she's every inch a movie star as she works the red carpet. The flash-bulbs are blinding in response.

"Hey, why didn't you ever mention your cousin Helen's secret identity?" You and Walter have been stationed to the side by one of Hunter's people, allowing you to talk for the first time out of her presence. "Don't you know how cool it is to have such a famous relative?" You've lived with Libby long enough to know that sharing a gene pool with Hunter will be Walter's ticket out of social Siberia.

"I guess I didn't really think about it," Walter says absently, reminding you yet again that he doesn't care what other people think of him. It's one of those traits you're sure will work out well for Walter in the long run. But this is high school. C'mon. Care a *little*? At least Walter had allowed Hunter to give him a mini-makeover before deplaning. His baggy sweater was ditched and the white oxford shirt underneath was rolled up to the elbows; his unruly mane of curls was tamed to John Mayer dimensions. Simple changes, but impactful. You have to admit, he looks—well, hot might be an overstatement. But *cute*. Definitely cute. It's a little weird, actually. You're seeing Walter as a *guy* for the first time tonight. And you're glad you ended up borrowing Annabel's hot Marc Jacobs mini.

"Now that that's over, let's have some fun," Hunter declares as she steps off the carpet. She grabs you and Walter each by an arm and pulls you toward the front door of the ultra-exclusive club where the party is taking place. The bouncer gets the velvet rope right out of her way and the three of you breeze inside. Hunter doesn't bother to thank him. Something about her has changed since you left New Hampshire, and you can tell that Walter's noticed it, too. Her movements are sharper, faster, and her face is more carefully composed—like she knows she's being watched every single moment. Which she is, of course. Watched, if not photographed. She chose an ironic stage name, given that she seems more the *hunted*.

Inside the dimly lit club, Hunter is immediately seized upon by a forty-something dude in a black button-down shirt. She makes no introduction, but you guess that he's the angry agent from the no-nonsense way he's whispering in her ear and pointing out key players around the room. "Be right back," she says, and then she's gone—leaving you and Walter to fend for yourselves.

Your eyes are still adjusting to the darkness. It was brighter on the street, thanks to the streetlamps, and about forty degrees cooler. The air inside Oberon is so dense and warm that your first impulse is to disrobe—no doubt, exactly the intention. Walter grabs your hand to lead you through the tightly packed crowd. As you gradually begin to see again, you scan for celebs. Could the leggy blonde on the dance floor be Cameron Diaz, rocking out? You're pretty sure Joe Jonas just did a shot at the bar. It's hard to tell—but tomorrow, when you're reliving this in the dining hall with the girls, it will be fact. You smile to yourself. Who would've guessed that a night that began with you missing out on Midwinter's would end with you partying in Manhattan?

"Martini?" asks a waiter, materializing next to you with a tray.

You look at Walter. You don't drink much, and he doesn't drink period. But tonight, perhaps to combat the strangeness of being air-dropped into this party, you take a martini and try a few sips. Definitely an acquired taste.

"The DJ is insane!" shouts Walter, and he's right—the music feels like it's pumping into every cell of your body like a drug. You grip his hand a little tighter. Is this what your twenties will be like, when you land that dream gig as a reporter for the *Times* and Walter's going for his philosophy Ph.D. at Columbia? (Natch, you've talked ten-year plans.) Walter is saying something else but you can't hear. On the fourth attempt, he pulls you close, his lips brushing ever so slightly against your ear. "You want to dance?"

That's when it happens. Without warning, your stomach does The Flip.

Uh-huh. The *Flip*! What does that mean?

Is it an "I'm at a sexy New York club having this unexpectedly fabulous night with my best guy friend whom I suddenly realize is cute" flip? Or is it a "my buddy just might have feelings for me and could cross the line and ruin our friendship if we hit the dance floor together" flip?

Good question. And one that only you can answer.

You are most likely to . . .

live a little. Get your groove on with Walter and that Cameron look-alike and see what happens next. Continue to Snapshot #20 (page 101).

or

put Walter off. You're seeing him with fresh eyes tonight, you have to admit—but you wouldn't want to lead him on or take a major risk with your friendship. Continue to Snapshot #21 (page 104).

Saturday, February 15, 9:35 p.m.
Main Street

The frigid air catches at the inside of your nose when you inhale; any second more snow will fall, blanketing Main Street. An old pickup truck pushing a paint-chipped snowplow goes by. The driver unrolls the window an inch to ash his cigarette and the ember lands just inches from your boot.

Staying on campus was the right call, you and Walter agreed, although a part of you wonders if you played it too safe by turning Hunter down. What's the point of being fourteen if not to occasionally break the rules in the name of fun? But then again, how much would it suck to be expelled from Kings, and watch all the opportunities in front of you get flushed down the drain? And so you'd said goodbye to Hunter—*Helen*—Hunter, and settled up the check. Walter would be right behind you in a minute. He'd bumped into some friends from the Debate Society and you'd told him to catch up with you on the walk back.

As you walk through the enormous wrought-iron gates that make the entrance to the Kings universe, you can't help but feel a massive case of FOMO—Fear of Missing Out.

Tonight, instead of having a blast at the biggest party of the year, you're stuck on the sidelines. Your friends will return home with juicy stories, while you'll have spent the evening eating greasy food and watching *Casablanca* with Walter . . . again. You could've hopped on a plane with a mega-celebrity, but you didn't have it in you to risk it. All in all, you feel like a bit of a dud.

Walter must have gotten caught up in conversation, because you're already at the Faculty Row—adorable white cottages where many of the younger teachers live, the ones who don't have families yet. You hear someone knocking furiously on a door. The streetlamps cast a sideways yellow glow, making it hard to see clearly, but you can make out a girl's silhouette on one of the porches.

"I know you're in there, Martin," she hisses between loud bangs. You immediately shiver: the voice unmistakably belongs to Oona de Campos. "You coward. At least come out and tell me like a man."

The door opens a sliver, but it's chained from the inside. It looks like Mr. Worth inside. "It's over between us, Oona."

Oona jams her body against the door, rocking the chain. "Since when? It didn't seem over last Thursday in your office!"

Mr. Worth covers his face with his hands. As much as you dislike Oona, you're suddenly filled with a shared rage toward Worth. So it's true—he really had a relationship with Oona, a sixteen-year-old student. It's one of those things you wish you could un-know, like the ingredients of a hot dog. You wouldn't have thought it possible that you'd feel a genuine sympathy for Oona de Campos. Last year Oona locked a freshman in the trophy case wearing only his tightie whities. She made poor Mademoiselle Fradette, the sweet French teacher with the bowl haircut, weep at her desk after class. Oona was not a kind person. But she didn't deserve this.

Something in your gut tells you that Martin Worth is even worse, and that this fling with him could only leave Oona more damaged, more bitter, more angry at the world. You're not sure the world can handle that.

"You need to calm down," says Mr. Worth in a patronizing tone. "Really, Oona, you're acting like a spoiled child right now. What we had was fun. You're a great girl, really—"

"Just tell me her name, douche bag! Tell me her name and I won't show Headmaster Fredericks the photo I have on my iPhone."

You can hear Worth gulp from where you're standing. That must be some photo. "Heather. Heather McPherson. Happy?"

"Oh, I'm ecstatic. Can't you tell?"

The door slams shut in her face, and for a moment Oona doesn't move. In her shearling coat and stiletto boots, she's a vision of sophistication—and yet her shoulders are shaking gently in quiet sobs. Oh, jeez. Oona is acting . . . human. The Queen of Mean is just a heartbroken teenage girl.

You are most likely to . . .

keep walking. It's none of your business. Besides, sometimes a wounded animal can be the most vicious. Continue to Snapshot #22 (page 108).

or

talk to her. She's obviously hurting . . . and who knows what she'll do to Mr. Worth's other woman. You're a girls' girl at heart, and you hate to see even Oona in so much pain. Continue to Snapshot #23 (page 112).

Saturday, February 15, 9:05 p.m.
Lakeshore Woods

"Libby's map says it should be just up ahead," says Spider, holding back the branch of a pine tree so it doesn't whack you in the face. She holds Walter's yellow flashlight—the only light you have, other than your iPhone screens—with her other hand. "You guys must be freezing." As usual, Spider's dressed in a pair of forest green exercise pants, KINGS printed in block letters down one leg, a gray hoodie, and a forest green knit cap with a soccer ball sewn on the front. You've all tried to coax her into girlier clothes, but it's no use. With her ski-jump nose and corkscrew curls, Spider still manages to look cute. And more important, warm. A miniskirt and bare legs on a freezing February night . . . what were you thinking?

"This party is pretty epic," says Libby, speaking loudly so that Hunter can hear every word. "Every February the seniors wheel in kegs, string up lanterns in the trees . . . it's been a Kings tradition since forever."

You can't help but feel a stab of secondhand embarrassment. Libby's talking up Midwinter's to a girl who went to last year's Oscars?

There's a growing twinkle of laughter from up ahead. Someone shrieks; a heavy bass thrums. Some boys start to chant something—you're still too far away to make out what they're saying. You blow into your hands before pulling out your makeshift flask, an old water bottle filled with rum and Coke. You take a sip, hoping it'll warm you up. For a moment, it does. Another sip. After the shots back in Pennyworth, you're starting to really feel it. It's not just the alcohol, of course—it's the excitement of being at an upperclassmen party with all your best friends, including Walter, and especially including Hunter. You can only imagine how everyone will freak when they realize she's part of your group.

You and Annabel are the first ones to the clearing, where an enormous fire blazes, warming the air. Heaven. You can feel your toes start to thaw. There are about fifty or so kids already partying, their cheeks flushed, and you feel like you've stumbled into a Ralph Lauren ad. At first, nobody seems to notice the arrival of your pack.

"Henry!" Annabel calls out, running to her boyfriend and lacing her long, slender arms around his neck. She holds on tight and he hugs her back. In the romantic flicker of the bonfire, they're a vision of perfection. Henry's eyes lift suddenly, catching you mid-stare. You look away immediately, face involuntarily turning scarlet.

There are some choices you make—what to wear, whether to study for your upcoming economics quiz or go out for pizza with your girls—and some that seem to be made for you. How you wish your feelings for Henry Dearborn were a choice. Instead it feels like they're a part of your hardwiring. Every time you look at those sandy curls, every time his brow furrows as he tries to come up with the right headline during a newspaper meeting, every time you pick up the phone and it's him, something deep inside you takes over, overriding the voice of reason telling you *bad idea.*

"There's the keg," Spider says, grabbing your hand and pulling you through the crowd. Walter and Hunter follow. Hunter looks amused by the scene—her smile is a little condescending, perhaps, but then again, she's not used to partying with kids her own age.

Traipsing behind Spider, you scan the crowd. There's Crosby Wells, leaning against a knocked-over tree trunk, holding court with some drama club girls. Genus: Pot-smoking bohemian/indie musician. Species: Hottie. The jocks, as usual, take up the most room, crashing into each other for unknown reasons in their faded baseball caps and Patagonia fleeces. You recognize Matthew Ramirez, the football quarterback, and Billy Grover, a hockey superstar. Libby's been obsessed with Billy for the past few weeks, ever since they made out at a party during winter finals. He hasn't called her since.

"Keep your cup," snaps a senior girl you vaguely recognize from school assemblies as she fills up your red plastic cup with foamy beer. She's clearly impressed with her position of importance as keg master. "Whoa, are you Hunter Mathieson?" she asks when it's Hunter's turn at the spigot. Heads swivel.

"That's what they tell me," Hunter responds, flashing Keg

Master a winning smile. She and Walter may share the same blue eyes, but they're pretty different when it comes to ego.

"I'm a huge fan." Keg Master has turned deferential now. She produces a Sharpie. "Would you sign my beer cup?" Hunter obliges, and by the time she's finished her signature, a crowd has gathered around her. Libby beams with pride, as though she discovered Hunter herself, and Walter remains at his cousin's side, an impromptu security guard for the night, buffering Hunter from her fans. Finally, he pulls her out of the fray and the three of you catch your breath at the edge of the party.

"Is this a typical Saturday night for you guys?" Hunter asks. The setting is as beautiful as anything Hollywood could produce. Seniors have strung the birch branches with delicate lanterns, transforming the clearing into a twinkling, enchanted place.

"I'm still not sure what's typical at Kings"—it's the truth; there's always something new around each corner—"but for Walter and me, Saturday night typically involves cheese fries." Walter laughs. You sip your beer.

Without meaning to, your eyes once again find Henry in the crowd—the way your hand might start to scratch before your brain realizes you had an itch. He's still standing next to Annabel, now talking with a few of his buddies. Her arms are wrapped around his waist, lightly, and every few seconds she nuzzles against him. It feels like something is squeezing your heart.

You're nearly finished with your beer when Oona de Campos saunters over, drop-dead gorgeous in a shearling coat with a glamorously high collar. You can't help but shiver. She alone acts completely unimpressed by Hunter's presence. Instead, she seems to be sniffing her out as a potential rival. But it's Walter she addresses. "Walter, is it? Walter, I hate to be the one to tell you, but this party is off-limits for freshman guys."

Hunter immediately takes the bait. "Who are you?"

"Oona de Campos. And who are you?"

Hunter gives a derisive laugh, as though it's too ridiculous to consider anyone not knowing exactly who she is. "Right. You can go away now."

You literally gasp. Nobody at Kings would ever dare to speak so rudely to Oona, and for a second, she's shocked speechless. But she quickly recovers, of course. "You do look familiar. Are you on one of those reality shows?"

Hunter rolls her eyes. "You got me."

"Well, in any case, I'm sorry you won't be able to stay." Oona's voice is pure velvety purr, but there's no mistaking her Declaration of War. As she stalks away to rejoin the girls who follow her every decree, there's no doubt that trouble is brewing.

"What a whack-job," sneers Hunter.

"We should hit the road, though," Walter says. "I didn't know—"

"We are so not doing that." Hunter suddenly shivers, pulling her cashmere scarf up over her chin. "I'm freezing. Let's warm up for a second." The three of you drift back closer to the fire, feeling its warmth in your extremities.

DeeDee Banks, one of Oona's minions, trots over. "Um, excuse me, but we're going to have to ask you to leave, like, now." She says this to the group but stares at the ground. "A rule is, um, a rule. No freshman guys."

Hunter pulls herself up to her full five feet three. "Tell your fearless leader over there to mind her own business." The petrified girl reports back.

You are most likely to . . .

→ join Hunter in standing up to Oona, and do what you can to overthrow the school bully. Walter shouldn't have to leave. Continue to Snapshot #24 (page 120).

or

→ stay out of the drama. Like you want to be on Oona's hit list? Walter really doesn't care about the party, anyway. Continue to Snapshot #25 (page 125).

SNAPSHOT #13

Saturday, February 15, 9:05 p.m.
Lakeshore Woods

"Libby's map says it should be just up ahead," says Spider, leading your little pack through the pitch-black woods with the flashlight Walter found in his room. "You guys must be freezing." You and she are the only ones dressed appropriately for the chilly February night. In her sporty wind pants and knit hat, Spider looks like she's going to a game and not a party. You'd had the good sense to change out of Annabel's outfit, throwing on some warm boots and a pair of jeans. Not as fashionable, but at least now you're not at risk for hypothermia.

Libby is waxing on about the Kings party scene (obviously her attempt to impress Hunter) when you hear the first notes of shrieked laughter and thumping music from up ahead. "We must be close," Walter says from the back of the group. You're glad he's here. Really glad. Having your best friends with you pretty much guarantees a great night.

The first person you see when you reach the clearing—which is wonderfully warm, thanks to the enormous bonfire,

64

and quite beautiful, thanks to the tiny lanterns strung through the trees—is Henry. The clearing is chaos, packed with kids, and yet your eyes are immediately pulled to Henry, like metal to a magnet. He's standing slightly apart from the crowd with some of his buddies, chuckling quietly over some shared joke. Annabel, who's been behind you through the woods, spots him and does what you can only dream of doing: she runs to him, throws her arms around his neck, and kisses him passionately.

It's painful to watch, so you quickly avert your eyes. You wish your best friend's happiness wasn't a torture, but there doesn't seem to be much you can do to change the way you feel. The best you can do is distract yourself. Maybe what you need is to find another guy—an *available* guy—to help you forget about the one you can't have.

"There's the keg," Spider says, grabbing your hand and pulling you through the crowd toward the keg, Walter and Hunter close behind. Libby has already found some field hockey friends and is taking swigs from a huge bottle of vodka they're passing around. You've tried, in the past, to get Libby to pace herself, but it never seems to work—which is why she's ended so many nights hugging the toilet at the end of the hallway.

Weaving through the noisy crowd, you scout for romantic prospects. Being lucky in love will take more than a few drops of blood, in your case—it will mean opening yourself up to the idea of other guys besides Henry.

Leaning against a fallen tree, there's Crosby Wells, the sexy and talented musician with longish dark hair, penetrating eyes, and confidence to spare. In the jock corner is Matthew Ramirez: football quarterback and all-around good guy, if a little square. He's standing with Billy Grover, the hockey player who Libby's been obsessed with since they kissed at a party, Dexter Trent, who's as amazing a soccer player as Spider is, and Hamilton Leeds—school president, super nice and bound for Yale in the fall, but not exactly crush material.

Crosby has potential, but he's intimidatingly cool. Besides, there's only one Henry Dearborn. Sucks to be you.

"Keep your cup," snaps the keg master, a bossy senior girl who reads the morning announcements in school-wide assemblies. "Whoa, are you Hunter Mathieson? You look exactly like her!" A crowd seems to gather immediately, and before long Hunter is busy autographing beer cups. Walter does his best to buffer her, but it soon becomes clear that Kings is full of die-hard Hunter fans. After a few frenzied minutes, he shouts, "That's it for autographs!" and pulls her to the relatively quiet edge of the party, where you and Spider breathlessly regroup.

"I'm sorry for the mob scene," Spider says. "I thought kids would be a little cooler."

"It's no big deal," says Hunter. She smiles but it's sort of empty. Being ordinary has its perks, you suddenly think.

You see Henry and Annabel in front of you, backlit by the flickering fire, deep in conversation, and your stomach drops. You just can't seem to avoid seeing them. Parties should be fun, but this one just isn't. Not for you. And just like that, your mind is made up. "I'm not feeling well," you tell your little group. "I think I've got to go home."

"Seriously?" Spider's face falls.

"Yeah, I'm just—feeling lousy. Dining hall fried clams, definitely the wrong call."

Spider squares her shoulders and nods. "Okay, then, let's get you home."

It's such a characteristic Spider response—no hesitation in leaving the party, if there's a friend in need—that you reach out and pull her into a hug. "You're the best. But I'm fine. I know exactly where I'm going." This may not be strictly true, but how hard can it be? You'll find your way back home—or maybe to Glory Days first, and then home. Cheese fries for one (instead of the party everyone will be talking about for weeks) is a new low, but you'd rather be there versus forced to witness the love fest between Annabel and Henry.

"No way you're going solo," Spider declares.

"We'll head back with her," Walter says, tuning in to the conversation. "Helen never ate dinner. I mean, Hunter. I can't get used to calling her that."

Maybe you don't have Henry Dearborn, but you do have some pretty amazing friends.

As you, Hunter, and Walter say goodbye to Spider and make your way out, something catches your eye. Billy Grover now has his arm wrapped tightly around Libby, who's well on her way to full-out drunk. She sways into him, one manicured hand pressing against his strong chest. You watch Billy give a nod to his buddy—some meathead in a Boston College baseball cap whose name you always forget. Boston College is pouring drinks for the group, mixing cranberry juice with vodka in plastic cups. It's hard to be sure since the flickering lanterns create a lot of shadows, but you could've sworn he slipped a pill into one of the cups before handing it over to Billy, who hands it over to . . . Libby. She immediately takes a sloshing sip.

You are most likely to . . .

charge over and grab the cup away from Libby. What if that was a roofie? Better safe than sorry. Continue to Snapshot #26 (page 131).

or

head back to campus. You're sure it was nothing. Libby will be fine—and if you interfere, she'd probably bite your head off for cramping her style with Billy. Continue to Snapshot #27 (page 134).

SNAPSHOT #14

Saturday, February 15, 8:45 p.m.
Lakeshore Woods

"I wonder if Billy's going tonight," Libby repeats for the third time since you left your cozy dorm room to brave the frigid wilderness. This time, nobody even bothers to answer her. You're all too busy watching your footing, which is precarious, given how hard it is to see by the dim light cast from your iPhone screens. All the tequila you drank back in the room doesn't help.

"What was that?" Annabel stops suddenly. "Are there coyotes in these woods?"

Before anyone can join her freak-out, you hear the sounds of the party up ahead. Some girls shriek at the top of their lungs. You can hear the heavy bass of the music. And then, slowly, the warm light of the bonfire comes into view, and you've arrived.

"Wow," says Libby, taking in the beautiful chaos with wide-eyed awe. You tug at your miniskirt a little, your legs completely covered in goose bumps. All the different pockets of Kings's social system are segregated around the enormous fire. The jocks are huddled on one side, closest to the kegs.

You notice hockey star Billy Grover, Libby's obsession du jour, joking around with varsity QB Matthew Ramirez. Crosby Wells, a cool, intriguing musician, is flocked by drama club girls and—well, girls in general. He's kind of a stud. School president Hamilton Leeds, overachiever among overachievers, is talking to his second-in-command, Margot Harris, about some matter of apparently urgent importance. Sometimes you wonder what rabbit hole you fell down to land in this world of privilege, where winter break plans usually require a passport and skis and most students' families own a minimum of three homes. These are your peers?

You spot Henry standing with a few of his buddies and feel the now predictable rush start from your stomach then hit your entire body. Henry transcends any one particular social label—he's a terrific lacrosse player but not too cool to hang with the nerd herd; he's really into journalism, but doesn't spend his free periods at the backstage of the auditorium with half the newspaper staff. He's not the kind of person who'd hide cowardly behind a closed door, letting a good friend stand alone on the other side of it. Looking at him, you feel a fresh wave of shame over how you treated Walter. As Annabel finds him and throws her arms around him, you turn away.

Spider's made her way to the keg, Libby's found her field hockey friends, and Annabel is now clenched in a lip-lock with the guy you love. Despite the throngs of drunk and semi-drunk kids around you, falling over, laughing too loudly over nothing funny, you feel completely alone.

If you can't beat 'em, join 'em.

The urge to get drunk—and stop thinking so damn much about Henry—hits you. You pull out your makeshift flask (a water bottle filled with rum, pilfered from Libby's parents' bar, and Coke) and drink. Halfway through the bottle, you start to feel a little wobbly. You look for Spider but she's not in the keg line anymore. Taking shot after shot from your flask, you wander through the crowd, looking for one of your room-mates, scanning for any familiar face. Before you know it, the bottle is empty and you haven't found a friend.

"Are you okay?" Someone puts a steadying hand on your arm and pulls you out of the current. You're surprised to see that it's Billy Grover. Libby's crush. You teeter slightly, jostled from behind, and fall against him. You leave your hand on his arm a moment too long, not quite able to find your balance.

"Oh, yeah. I guess I'm just kind of a lightweight." You hope the words only sound so slurred in your head.

"Here, why don't you sit down?" Billy guides you over to an area where some of his meathead buddies are gathered, a pit of backward baseball caps and guys chewing tobacco. Something in his eyes tells you that it won't be long before he's trying to hook up. Even in your current state, you know Libby would be apoplectic if she found you with Billy. But then you remember how she pushed you to diss Walter. Would it serve her right?

You are most likely to . . .

take a seat next to Billy. Libby's not the boss of you . . . and you feel too wobbly to stay upright. Continue to Snapshot #28 (page 142).

or

keep searching for a friend—preferably one who can help take care of you. Leave Billy to Libby. Two wrongs don't make a right. Continue to Snapshot #29 (page 146).

SNAPSHOT #15

Saturday, February 15, 8:45 p.m.
Lakeshore Woods

"Do you think Billy's seeing someone? Or maybe he has a new phone and my texts didn't go through," says Libby, swatting wildly at pine branches with both of her hands. Had the girl ever been in the woods before? And could she hear herself speak? You make a mental note to anonymously slip a copy of *He's Just Not That Into You* into her mailbox.

"My sister Caroline knew his older brother Jackson," Annabel says, choosing her words carefully. "He was a year ahead of her. She, um, doesn't have the greatest things to say about him. Apparently he was kind of terrible to girls—"

"Well, that's his brother," Libby interrupts. "Billy's been nothing but super-sweet."

Like when he super-sweetly jammed his tongue down Libby's throat for two hours at the winter finals party and then never called her again? Libby may be on the dean's list, but in some ways she can be frighteningly dumb. You're still pissed at her for pushing you to desert Walter. Would including him really have been such a big deal? Now everything she

73

does and says seems to lodge right under your skin. Maybe you should have taken a shot, just to take the edge off your black mood.

"Hey, watch it!" A supple branch escapes from Libby's hand and swings back to hit you in the face. It doesn't hurt, really, but you're secretly glad for the excuse to yell at her.

"Sorry, sorry—I can't see a thing!" Since none of you have a flashlight, you're inching your way single file through the woods with only the light of your phones illuminating the path.

"Get behind me, then!" you snap, hurrying forward when she steps to the side of the path.

"I don't know what you're so mad about," Libby mutters as you pass. "Just because I didn't feel like showing up with dweeby Walter—"

"Walter is not dweeby!" you yell back.

"Libby, come on. He's not." Annabel's stern tone shuts her right up. The four of you walk in silence for a little bit. Is it your imagination, or does Annabel seem upset about something? Other than helping you get dressed, she's been pretty aloof all day.

"New text!" Libby shrieks, clinging to the ridiculous hope that it might be Billy. As she's looking at her screen, her foot catches on a root. Before you can brace yourself she's knocked right into you, sending you careening into Spider. You hear a thud and a dull crack as all three of you hit the ground, phones sailing in all directions. It's like a game of human dominoes, with only Annabel left standing on the narrow winding path.

Without even the small light of your screens, you're enveloped in total darkness.

"Are you guys okay?" asks Annabel breathlessly from above you. Ouch. Your palms were badly scraped from the fall.

"I ripped my tights! How am I going to show up like this?" Libby pouts. She begins to search for her phone. No apology, no nothing. You seriously want to kill her.

"Are *you* okay, Spider?" you ask pointedly, getting up. She's still on the ground, and she's holding her leg tightly. You step closer and she lets out an involuntary whimper. "Did you hurt your leg?"

"Shit," says Spider in a tight voice. You try to help her get vertical, but she can't put weight on the injured leg. "I landed weird." Spider's voice sounds like she's forcing words out through enormous pain. For a moment you're glad it's dark, so she can't see the panic on your face.

Annabel takes charge. "Okay, we've got to get her to the hospital. I'll take Spider's legs and you guys take her shoulders. We'll have to carry you out, Spider, and we'll do our best not to jostle your leg too much. I'll call an ambulance and have them meet us right at the trailhead."

You slip your arm under Spider's and link at the elbow with Libby, forming a hammock. Nobody talks, but everyone is thinking the same thing: a broken bone could sideline Spider for the entire spring season. Spider without sports is like Spider without oxygen.

You've been shuffling along for about ten minutes when you realize that Spider is crying.

"Are you in terrible pain?" you ask, your heart in your throat. Poor girl. Spider is incredibly tough, so the tears must mean the pain is excruciating.

"No, I'm just—you guys, if I can't play sports, I don't know if I'll even be able to stay here at Kings." Spider speaks quickly, the words rushing out of her like air from a balloon. "I didn't want to tell you guys this, it's embarrassing, but I've been on academic probation since last semester." Spider hangs her head a little. "Coach had to beg for me to get another chance. And my parents completely freaked. See, if my GPA isn't up at the midterm, I'll lose my scholarship. It's not really about the money. If they wanted to, my parents could cover the tuition. But since they think I'm being lazy, or whatever, they won't. They don't understand how hard this school is. I'm not smart enough to go here, you guys, and that's the bottom line. And if I can't play, it's not like the school will want me here either." It's so strange to hear Spider cry, it actually gives you goose bumps. You and Libby give her a squeeze.

You're the first to speak. "Spider, I can't believe you've had all this on your shoulders and haven't said anything! You know we'll all do whatever we can to help you with your grades. We'll get you through this, I promise."

"Absolutely," Libby seconds, and for a second, you stop hating her.

"We all know how hard it is," Annabel adds. "Everyone needs help at times. Nothing embarrassing about *that*."

A moment later, you can just barely make out the headlights of the ambulance Annabel called. None of you talk about what will happen next. How will you explain being out in the middle of the woods at ten o'clock at night? No story seems plausible. But the important thing is getting Spider to the hospital.

Cars whiz by on the road. Up ahead the ambulance comes into view, along with three EMTs and . . . Headmaster Fredericks. Of course he'd be alerted when a Kings student called for an ambulance pickup in the middle of nowhere. Your stomach drops. Even from here you can tell that he's pissed. "You girls had better tell me what's going on, you'd better tell me the truth, and you'd better tell me *now*," he barks as Spider is loaded onto the stretcher.

You are most likely to . . .

→ spill it. Ratting out the party is social suicide, no question about it, but it's still better than expulsion. Continue to Snapshot #30 (page 151).

or

→ cook up some story about going for a midnight hike as a roommate bonding experience, and pray he buys it. Continue to Snapshot #31 (page 154).

SNAPSHOT #16

Saturday, February 15, 11:30 p.m.
Pennyworth House

Annabel is sound asleep by *SNL*'s Weekend Update, as usual. Tonight you're grateful she's out cold, for her sake as well as your own. Her eyes are red and puffy from crying. You can only imagine how excruciating the breakup has been for her. Henry is her first love, and Annabel had hoped he'd be hers forever. Naïve, perhaps, but you understand it completely. Who wouldn't want to be with Henry forever?

You scoop up the tear-sodden tissues surrounding her on the couch, dumping them in the garbage basket, before realizing that your own eyes are brimming over with tears. Have you made a terrible mistake by promising to never let anything happen with Henry? It seemed like the right—really, the only—thing to do when confronted with Annabel's misery. But as soon as the words "I promise" left your lips, you'd felt a heavy ache around your heart. Now it feels like you're mourning the end of a relationship that never even had a chance to begin. And you feel a deep frustration, too, knowing that there was a chance to be with the guy of your dreams—but it just didn't work out for you.

Because of Annabel.

You glance at your sleeping best friend, feeling a surge of resentment toward her. For Annabel's entire life, she's had everything handed to her. She's always gotten whatever she wanted, and easily. Is her sadness in losing Henry really about heartbreak—or is it the reaction of a girl who's used to having her own way? You've never before thought of Annabel as spoiled, not really—but isn't she? Even her generosity suddenly feels cast in a new light. How hard is it to share some of your clothes when you're getting new ones every single month, and more than one girl could possibly wear? When you have Daddy's AmEx and can head to Boston for a shopping spree with Libby any time the mood strikes?

When Libby tiptoes in, careful not to wake the RA, you're glad to be distracted from these thoughts. "How was the party?" you ask.

Libby glances over at Annabel's sleeping form. "Well, we hate Billy Grover. And double-hate Oona de Campos. They were all over each other in the most revolting way."

"I don't know what you ever saw in him," you say. "But those two deserve each other."

She snuggles in next to you on the couch, Annabel on the other side. "Taylor Swift is hosting?" Libby whispers, reaching into your bag of salt and pepper Popchips. "Can she stop with the cheesy floral dresses?"

"She's playing a part, Lib," you say, taking a chip. "It's a sketch."

"You know she'd rock that look in real life."

"Hey, speaking of weird outfits, what was up with Margot's sequined pants? Sequins in the woods?" Not that you have any right to play fashion police, but it feels good to talk about nothing. To let yourself be distracted by gossip. To stop skewering Annabel in your mind.

"Certifiable. Oh"—Libby slaps your arm—"I meant to tell you, Crosby Wells looked forlorn when you left. And he asked Spider for your last name. He's totally gonna call you!"

Crosby. You try to muster up some of the excitement you'd felt about him earlier in the evening. Maybe tomorrow, after some sleep, you'll feel it again. Tomorrow, when you start to figure out how to forget about Henry, forget about the possibility that something could've sparked between the two of you.

"Where's Spider?" Strange that Libby beat her home.

"No clue." Libby pulls out her phone and dispatches a text. "She wasn't there when I left. The secret life of Spider Harris. Have you noticed she's been acting a little strange lately? I mean, stranger than usual."

"What do you mean?"

"I don't know. Just secretive. She always jumps when I come into the bedroom."

"Maybe she just wants some privacy." Maybe, like you, Spider occasionally craves having a moment to herself. You love having roommates, but it can get overwhelming to have someone there all the time. For an only child, it's been an adjustment. You stretch your legs out on the glossy enamel coffee table that Mrs. Monroe's decorator had flown in from a boutique in L.A.

"Maybe," Libby says. "But I think she's hiding something."

Aren't we all? you wonder. Annabel stirs in her sleep, disturbed by a bad dream. *Really, aren't we all?*

The End

SNAPSHOT #17

Sunday, February 16, 10:14 a.m.
Hamilton Dining Hall

At first, you think it must be in your head. How could your friends turn on you so immediately? Tommy and Lila act like they don't see you in line at the omelet station and hurry off to fill up their coffee mugs. When you call to them, they give a wan "oh hey" before heading to check out. Maybe they're tired, you think. Hung over. But when you follow them to a table and sit down next to Lila—just like you'd do any other morning—they exchange weird glances and decide to take their coffee "to go." They hustle away. The dining hall is filling up, but you sit alone.

Get used to solitary, kid.

Let's back up twelve hours, to that awkward moment in the woods when you were forced to choose between your loyalty to Annabel and your own happiness. You'd tried your best to put off an answer, but she'd pressed. Finally you'd told her that, of course, you would never jump into something with Henry—if he really was interested, which was a humongous if. That didn't satisfy Annabel. She'd once again demanded that you promise you'd *never* be with him. Never? All you'd done was repeat the word, and she'd flown into hysterics.

"Why can't you promise? Are you in love with him, too?" She was sputtering mad, a state you'd never imagined seeing Annabel in. "Did anything ever happen between the two of you?"

"Of course not!"

But it was too late, and beside the point. Annabel couldn't even look at you. She'd sprinted off through the woods, and this time you had no hope of catching up to her.

Apparently she'd called Libby on the way, as your other roommate seemed to arrive on your heels back at Pennyworth. "Do not even speak to me!" Libby had bellowed in your direction when she barged through the door to find you in the common room and Annabel locked in your shared bedroom. "You are such a bitch." She raced over to her bedroom door. "Annie? It's me, sweetie." The door immediately unlocked and you could see Annabel on the other side, face red and blotchy from crying. You stayed on the couch, because really, what else could you do?

Would it have been better to lie to Annabel? Or make a false promise?

Earlier that morning, before heading to the dining hall to be shunned by Tommy and Lila, you'd passed Spider in the hallway on the way to the bathroom. "I heard about what happened," she'd said with a sad, puzzled look on her face. "I know you were just trying to be honest, but really, Annabel is so hurt."

It hits you that you've made a terrible choice. A hurtful choice. You should have reassured Annabel—that's what she needed, clearly—and then revisited the question down the road, once she'd had a chance to recover. Maybe it wouldn't have been fully honest, but you should've given her time to heal before even opening up the possibility you'd date her ex. It's obvious now. But the damage has already been done. And you're already feeling the loss of your best friend, and you couldn't imagine any breakup feeling worse.

Alone at a long dining hall table, you manage to get down a few bites of scrambled eggs before your phone buzzes with a text message. You glance down at the screen to find it's from Henry, stopping your heart for a moment.

> Glory Days in 15 minutes?
> —Henry

Heart in your throat, your fingers quickly type back that you'll see him there.

Will love bloom? Continue to Snapshot #17A (page 85) to find out.

Sunday, February 16, 10:35 a.m.
Glory Days Diner

In the narrow alley between Glory Days and the bookstore,
you pause to smooth your hair and calm your nerves. What
will you and Henry say to each other? Could Annabel's suspicions be correct? You pray that nobody sees you and Henry
together. It would be the final nail in the coffin of your friendship with Annabel. Bracing yourself, you force yourself
through the doors of the diner, immediately spotting Henry
in one of the booths. Like you, it looks like he didn't sleep
much the night before.

"Hey," he says as you slide into the other side of the booth.
"Rough night, huh? Thanks for meeting me."

"Of course," you tell him. "How are you doing?"

"I've been better. How's Annabel?"

"Upset, the last time I checked." *With both of us,* you don't
add.

Your answer must not come as any surprise, and yet hearing it out loud makes Henry cringe. "I never wanted to hurt
her."

You feel disloyal discussing Annabel any further. You certainly don't want to make her sound pitiful, or heartbroken. "I'm sure Annabel just needs a little time, that's all," you say, as though you've got all the experience in the world to back this up.

Henry looks a little relieved. "Of course." He clears his throat. "Um, did she happen to mention why we broke up?"

Here it is: the question that had weighed on your mind all night. Is Henry interested in you? Did you break up your best friend's relationship?

"Not really," you say. "She just said you wanted to see other people."

Henry nods slowly, choosing his words. "The truth is, there's one other person I've been thinking about. For a while now." His eyes meet yours directly and you have your answer. Henry Dearborn is talking about you. It feels like all the oxygen has been sucked out of the diner. "I don't want to put you in an uncomfortable spot, but I need to tell you how I feel—"

"Henry, don't." You stop him mid-confession, reaching across the table to touch his hand. "Listen, I'm incredibly flattered. And I, you know, in any other circumstances, would be thrilled. But Annabel is really important to me. Her feelings have to come first right now."

"I thought you'd say that. No, I *knew* you would. One of the things I like about you is your loyalty to your friends. I hope you're not mad at me for bringing it up."

"I'm anything but mad."

"If you feel uncomfortable, you know, working together at the newspaper, you can switch editors." Henry looks forlorn. "Of course I'd understand."

"Henry, we're still friends. And I'm not giving up the best editor on staff. Sorry, you're stuck with me."

Betty, your third-favorite waitress, comes over to take your order. "The usual?" she asks, refilling Henry's coffee cup.

"You have a usual?" Henry smiles. "What is it?"

"Don't judge." You point to the menu. "The Big Boy special. Pancakes, eggs, and hash browns."

"Impressive." He laughs.

Betty taps her order pad with her pencil, impatient despite the fact that the diner is otherwise completely empty.

"Actually, I should probably go," you tell Henry. It doesn't feel right to sit here enjoying breakfast with the guy who— whether he meant to or not—broke Annabel's heart last night.

"No problem. I'll see you at Tuesday's meeting."

You give him a mini-salute and head out the door, feeling much lighter than you did walking in. You've both said what you needed to say. You feel good about where things stand. And you can't help but feel buoyed by Henry's feelings for you. Maybe, down the line, once Annabel is recovered and the sting is gone, you and Henry can pick up this conversation again and see where it takes you. But for now, you've got a friendship to mend.

→ *Continue to Snapshot #17B (page 88).*

Thursday, June 5, 9:05 p.m.
Outside of Pennyworth House

Your dad helps you lug your last duffel bag down to the station wagon. The Quad is teeming with parents, most of whom brought some "extra hands" to deal with the manual labor of moving their kids out of the dorms. Freshman year is officially over, hard as that is to believe. Time to head home to a relaxing summer of reading in the hammock and working at a kids' camp. You never thought you'd be so excited to be back in your hometown, but it'll be the perfect antidote to a stressful—or at least, eventful—spring semester.

"Okay if I just run up and say goodbye to the girls?" you ask, and your dad waves you off, rearranging your stuff in the backseat so the car doors will actually close. Mom couldn't get the day off, so you'll see her in a few hours.

During the past few months, you've put a great deal of effort into recovering your friendship with Annabel. Things will never be exactly the way they were, but at least the friendship is intact. Once Annabel accepted your apology, so did your other friends. You'll never forget how immediately most of them sided with her—not even bothering to hear your side

88

of the story. But you're not sure you blame them. Choosing Henry over Annabel would have been incredibly insensitive, even cruel, to a friend who had never been anything but kind and giving to you.

"You leaving, kid?" Spider asks as she passes you on the stairs, her arms struggling to hold on to a giant cardboard box. She drops it to the ground and gives you a huge hug. "I'm coming to visit this summer, as soon as the clinics end." Spider's summer involves weeks of intensive training camps for her various sports. She'll be flying all over the country to work with the best coaches.

"You'd better," you answer, knowing you'll find some way out of it when the time comes. Hope Falls may be home sweet home, but you're not sure that you'd be comfortable having Spider visit. The thought alone makes you feel vulnerable. For one thing, there's not much to do. And even though Spider's super down-to-earth and would never judge, you don't relish the thought of anyone from Kings seeing your family's tiny home, or the rundown town, or the little grocery store where your mother works as a cashier. Why let them in on your little secret—that no matter how much you act like you belong at Kings Academy, you're faking it. You're from a different world.

Up in the room, Libby is bossing around two professional movers. You interrupt her to say goodbye, and she gives you a squeeze and a kiss on each cheek. There's no denying that Libby no longer feels like much of a friend, and you're sure she feels the same, but there's also no point to not being *friendly*.

Inside your shared bedroom, Annabel is neatly folding her clothes and laying them in neat stacks inside her T. Anthony monogrammed trunk. "I'm going to miss our room," she says, and you suddenly feel sentimental, too. The two of you have had so many heart-to-hearts in these bunk beds. You've started so many fun nights blasting music and getting ready together in the cramped space, sharing that floor-length mirror on the closet door. For all the ups and downs of this year, you'll look back and miss the time you spent here with Annabel. After all, she's the reason you decided to walk away from Henry. A decision you've never regretted, not even on those long nights working on the newspaper when you could feel his presence across the room.

"Will you call me when you get home, Annabel?" you ask, hugging her. "It's going to be so weird falling asleep tonight in my old room, without our usual pillow talk."

"Tell me about it."

Lately Annabel's been talking about a cute guy she'll see this summer up in Maine. She seems pretty excited about him. Who knows? Maybe your time with Henry will come sooner than you think.

The End

SNAPSHOT #18

Saturday, February 15, 10:20 p.m.
Moynihan Court

"**I wrote this song last summer in Southampton,**" says Crosby, pulling out yet another guitar. His room in Moynihan is smaller than yours, but a much-coveted single. He's crammed every square inch with musical equipment, instruments, and concert posters—cool stuff, but you have to admit the sheer volume is making you feel a little claustrophobic. Or maybe that's just your nerves. You've never been alone in a guy's room before—except Walter's, of course, but that doesn't exactly count. "It was inspired by a girl I met. We had this hot fling, but then her family went back to Texas and we never saw each other again."

Hot fling? You're not sure how to respond. It seems like TMI about another girl, but you try to let it go as he plays the first notes of "Everybody Thinks They Know Her," your favorite Dog Named Rex tune, on his guitar. Or close to it—the melody's close to the same, he's just changed the lyrics. Crosby's hands move easily over the strings, and he starts singing. Wow. His voice is really good—maybe not third round of

American Idol good, but good. You can't believe Crosby Wells is giving you a private concert. You try to ignore that his lyrics tell the story of a smoking-hot chick he couldn't get out of his head. Crosby croons about rolling around in sand dunes and skinny-dipping at Cooper's Beach. When he starts singing about taking off the girl's white bikini top, you can feel your cheeks turning red.

"What do you think?" he asks when the song's done, patting a spot next to him on the tapestry-covered bed. "Hey, you're so far away."

"You're really talented," you say, because it's true, and you perch next to him. It's hard to pinpoint the exact cause of your nervousness. It's hard to feel special when he's just finished singing about another girl. Or are you just feeling jumpy because you're interested in him? Is it the foreignness of being alone in a guy's room? A hot senior's room, no less?

"Thank you," he says, lighting up at the compliment. "What'd you think of the song itself? I've been writing more of my own material."

"You mean the lyrics?" You feel awkward answering that question. "It, um, sounds like you were really into her."

"Who?"

"The girl in the song. In the—um—'white string bikini' girl." You wish you could dive under one of his tapestries to hide your scarlet cheeks.

Crosby nods as though he hadn't considered this. "I met

her for a reason. This song needed to be born. Everything is inspiration for my music."

"So if you like Dog Named Rex," you say, changing the subject before he can make another pretentious statement, "you might like this killer band I heard in Providence last summer—"

"How'd you know I like Dog Named Rex?" Crosby looks slightly puzzled.

"Oh, just—the song?"

Now he looks thoroughly perplexed. "What about the song?"

"Um, isn't it kind of the same melody as 'Everybody Thinks They Know Her'?"

Crosby jumps up from the bed and storms over to the iPod dock, brow furrowed. "What are you talking about? It's not"—he fiddles to find the right song and then cranks up the volume. The unmistakable chorus echoes through the room. His eyes widen as the realization sinks in. "Shit," he says. "Shit, shit, shit." He runs his hands through his longish hair. "I begged my father to send the demo to his friend at Sony!" Rushing to his desk, he begins frantically dialing numbers. "Dad? Sorry, sorry to wake you . . . Sorry, I had no idea you were in London . . . Dad, tell me you didn't send that song to Dirk yet!"

He's forgotten that you're even there. Your first kiss less than an hour before—and now you're invisible to him. As Crosby pants into the phone, you stand up and make your way to the door. What else is there to do? Crosby doesn't bother to acknowledge your departure. Wow.

It's hard not to feel like a complete loser as you head home. You're just trudging up the stairs to Pennyworth when Henry Dearborn swings open the heavy oak front door. He looks very upset, and when he sees you, he forces a smile.

"Is Annabel okay?" you ask.

"Um, yeah, she's upstairs." Henry hurries past you down the stairs, then looks back over his shoulder. "I'm sorry I acted so weird earlier. It's none of my business if you and Crosby—"

"Oh, that went nowhere." You're glad it didn't, you realize, even if it was a blow to your ego. Sooner or later you would've realized that Crosby didn't care about you. Better sooner than later. "I'll see you Tuesday at the meeting."

"Right." Henry nods and shoves his hands in his pockets. "Crosby's not a bad guy. A little self-absorbed, maybe, but not a bad guy. I just think you deserve better. You deserve someone who really appreciates you."

Before you can respond, Henry disappears into the darkness of the Quad. His short pep talk leaves you with lighter spirits—and some strange new thoughts bouncing around your head. Thoughts about what really happened back at the bonfire. About why Annabel might've gotten so upset.

And so when you head upstairs to find Annabel bawling her eyes out on the couch, balled-up Kleenex surrounding her on all sides, you're not too surprised. Even though it defies the laws of reason, you're pretty sure Henry broke up with Annabel because he has something for you. You can just feel it. It explains his reaction to seeing you with Crosby. It might even explain why he's been assigned to edit every article you write for the newspaper—perhaps it was at his request. And even though it makes you feel like a terrible person, the thought is thrilling on an involuntary level. Being with Henry is a dream you've never fully allowed yourself to entertain. Not that it's going to happen. It would devastate your best friend. It's one thing to go through a breakup—quite another to watch helplessly from the sidelines as your ex gets together with your best friend. Still, just knowing Henry might like you is exhilarating.

You shake your head, trying to clear it. Maybe you can't control how you feel, but you can control what you *do*. You can be the friend Annabel needs you to be right now. "Are you okay?" you ask, sinking next to her on the couch and draping an arm over her shoulders.

"Not really," she says. "Henry and I broke up. It's crazy. Everything seemed to unravel so quickly."

"Do you want to talk about it?"

"Maybe tomorrow. I'm so exhausted right now, I can barely form words. You talk. Tell me about Crosby. What happened after I left? You guys would make a cute couple, you know."

You dutifully fill her in, including the disappointing ending.

"I guess Libby's love curse was a hoax," Annabel mutters,

resting her head back against a couch pillow. "Seriously, could either of us have been *less* lucky in love tonight?"

You nod, but a small part of you wonders whether your luck is looking up. Maybe someday, when Annabel is fully recovered from the breakup, you just might get your shot at being with the guy of your dreams.

The End

SNAPSHOT #19

Saturday, February 15, 10:05 p.m.
Lakeshore Woods

"Spider! Wait up!" You hurry over to the edge of the path, grabbing your friend's shoulder before she slips off into the dark woods by herself. You've just passed on Crosby's invitation back to his room. He was moving so fast, plus your brain can't seem to veer off thoughts of Henry. If it's meant to be, you'll get another chance with Crosby. "Are you leaving?"

Spider looks super flustered. "Oh, um—I was, yeah."

"By yourself? Hang on, I'll walk home with you." You have no big reason to stay at the party, especially minus Annabel and now Spider. But is it your imagination, or does Spider look less than thrilled that you'll be keeping her company?

It must be all in your head. Why would your friend want to trudge through the creepy dark woods solo?

As the two of you set off, Spider is uncharacteristically quiet, leaving you to jabber on about the party. She checks her phone as you walk, as though expecting to hear from someone. When you finally reach campus, you turn in the direction of Pennyworth—but Spider doesn't.

"Um, the thing is"—she kicks some pebbles—"I'm actually heading over to Moynihan to meet up with someone. A friend. Well, maybe more. I'm not sure, you know?"

Ah!

Now you know what this is about.

She looks so uncomfortable, you just want to reach out and pull her into a hug. This is a huge moment. You can hear what she's not saying: that she's going to meet a *girl*friend. Why else would she seem uncomfortable talking about her plans? Spider may be ready to come out of the closet to you, but it's up to you to make sure she feels supported. "Is this friend anyone I know?" you ask, trying to help her along.

"Maybe, I don't know."

"Well, whoever she is, I'm sure she's awesome." There. You said it so she wouldn't have to. So she would know you were totally cool with—

"*She?*" Spider's eyes pop with a combination of shock and amusement. "I'm meeting up with Dexter Trent. He's on the guys' soccer team. We're trying to keep it hush-hush so the rest of our teammates don't make a huge deal out of it. Did you think I was gay?"

"I didn't think anything, really—I just didn't know."

Spider bursts out laughing. "Just because I'm a jock who doesn't squeeze into stilettos or push-up bras every Saturday night doesn't mean I'm a lesbian. Come on, kid, way to stereotype!"

"It's just that you've never talked about guys before! Listen, it's not like it matters to me one way or the other. I just thought you might be."

"Well, you're right that I don't have a lot of experience with guys." She's back to looking nervous. "Dexter is awesome, but I'm kind of freaking out. I have no idea what he's expecting me to, like, do . . ."

You nod, now understanding the true cause of her discomfort. Your super-confident roommate is out of her comfort zone. "It doesn't matter what he's expecting, Spider. What matters is that you feel comfortable. That can be just talking, you know. You call the shots, Spider."

"I guess so." She shuffles her feet a little. "I just feel weird, knocking on his door. But he texted me to come over."

"Why don't you tell him to meet you at Glory Days instead?"

"I told you, we really don't want word getting out that anything's happening between us. The girls on the team would be merciless about it."

You can see her point. Other than playing soccer, the team's favorite activities seemed to be teasing, hazing, and ceaselessly making fun of each other. "Well, invite him over to our room. You guys can hang in the common room. I'll hit Glory Days and give you some privacy. I'm sure Annabel is at Henry's."

"Seriously?" You can see that Spider feels instantly relieved at the thought of being on her turf. "Okay, I'm gonna do that." She quickly punches the text into her phone. "You're sure you don't mind killing time at the diner? I feel bad, kicking you out. You can totally hang with us, too, you know. I mean, if he even wants to come over." Her phone bleats with a new text, and as she reads it, her face lights up in a huge grin. "He'll be there in twenty!"

You put an arm over her shoulders and the two of you happily continue on the path to Pennyworth. "You call the shots, Spider," you remind her before peeling off in the direction of cheese fries and a milk shake.

And so do you. Just because Crosby was into you and moving quickly didn't mean you had to rush into something with him. It gives you a surge of confidence, knowing that you stayed true to yourself and didn't just let a hot senior guy decide where the night would take you. It took some real strength to make that choice.

The End

SNAPSHOT #20

Sunday, February 16, 12:04 a.m.
Oberon

The dance floor is packed tight, but you and Walter manage to find a spot in what appears to be a grove of models. Eye level with Walter, they tower above you in teetering stilettos and sample-size dresses, their gazelle-like limbs moving perfectly in time to the beat. So what if they're stunning, you think to yourself, standing up straighter in your Steve Maddens. That's, like, their job. They probably don't have a brain in their heads. They probably—

"Did you read Friedman's op-ed this morning?" you can't help but overhear one of the models ask her friend. Her skin is as smooth and polished as ebony, and her head is practically shaved—a look that only the truly beautiful can pull off.

"Yeah, but I'm not sure I agree with him about pulling all aid to Pakistan. He completely equates the ISI with the Pakistani government, which I'm not convinced is entirely fair."

Oh, shut up, models.

"Are you having fun?" Walter asks, not seeming to notice the Glamazons surrounding him. To your surprise, he grabs you and pulls you close. To your greater surprise, you like it. You can smell soap on his skin. Dove. You use the same kind, but the scent is somehow different on him. "You look really pretty tonight, by the way," he says.

There it is again. Le Flip, Part Deux.

Walter's a good dancer, you realize, following his rhythm. There's so little space, your bodies are forced to touch. It's bizarre how unbizarre it feels. How easy it is to forget that Walter is *Walter*. Maybe it's that you've had too much martini, but when you slip your arms around his neck and the new Kanye song starts up, it feels right . . . and kind of exciting. Could you actually be feeling a romantic spark with your best guy friend?

Before you can make sense of the question, he ambushes you with a kiss.

"What are you doing?" You pull back, even though the kiss felt surprisingly good. Not too soft, not too hard. In fact, perfect—it was the perfect first kiss. Even better than you'd expected your first kiss to feel.

"Kissing you." Walter gives a funny little smile, his blue eyes twinkling.

"You can't just do that! What about our friendship?" It's the first time you've ever kissed a boy, not counting a few dry pecks at summer camp. You wonder if Walter has ever kissed anyone before. You wouldn't have thought so, but then it seemed like he knew what he was doing. Even now, he seems confident and calm. Neither of you is dancing anymore, the only stationary bodies on the throbbing dance floor.

"You know I'm crazy about you," Walter says, looking deep into your eyes.

Could best guy friend + great kisser = match made in heaven? Maybe . . . but what happens when you're back on campus? Should you factor in the reaction of your friends and the cool crowd?

You are most likely to . . .

kiss him back. You kind of just . . . want to. Why overthink it? Continue to Snapshot #37 (page 177).

or

hit the pause button. You're just not sure how you feel. Continue to Snapshot #38 (page 186).

SNAPSHOT #21

Sunday, February 16, 12:14 a.m.
Oberon

Walter had made no attempt to hide his disappointment when you put off dancing. Clearly he understood—you both knew—the subtext: you just wanted to be friends. To escape the awkwardness, you'd fled to the ladies' room, which was as much of a scene as the dance floor and just as shadowy, forcing girls to wiggle close to the mirror to check out their makeup.

"Did you see Hunter Mathieson out there?" It's impossible not to overhear the girl next to you talking to her two friends. She's wearing a skintight black leather dress that seems to be choking the life out of her. Her face is pale and drawn.

"Uh-huh. She looks awful. That girl is a walking pile of no." Tough crowd. You thought Hunter looked pretty smoking.

"At least she's lost the chunk," sniffs Leather Dress.

"You *know* it's the Lindsay Lohan circa 2007 diet."

"Ah." Her friend closes up her purse and gives her friend a meaningful look. "Next stop, Betty Ford." And then they're gone, receded back into the shadows, as you make sense of what they're insinuating about Walter's cousin.

Were they just haters . . . or could Hunter have a drug problem? Now that you think about it, she did make a bunch of trips to the bathroom during your short flight from New Hampshire. You'd already noticed that her demeanor had notably changed as the night progressed—she seemed to become more animated and more distant at the same time. And she was looking awfully skinny. You hadn't noticed at Glory Days, because she'd been bundled in layers, but once Hunter shed down to her dress, she was unexpectedly tiny. But weren't all starlets? You kind of assumed that everyone famous lived on cantaloupe and iced tea and worked out three hours a day.

Should you say something to Walter? Or is it just an empty rumor—the kind that could stir up a lot of unnecessary drama? You know exactly how he feels about drugs—the two of you have spent hours, if not days, thinking up ways to educate the Kings student body about their dangers.

Walter's no longer waiting for you by the huge pillar outside the ladies' room. You scan the crowd for him, feeling lost in the swank club. Thankfully, he hasn't drifted far. You spot him over by the bar with his back to you. As you approach, you find him engrossed in conversation with a redheaded model. Something clenches a little inside you when you realize just how gorgeous she is. Skin the color of fresh cream, stunning Titian hair, perfect little features. You've seen her before, in one of Libby's *Vogues*, or something.

"This is Carly," Walter says, introducing you. Carly gives you a fake-friendly smile that fools only Walter. When you stick out your hand, she pulls you in for a double air-kiss, Euro style. She smells like Chanel No. 5, just like Annabel's mother. "She just moved here from Kansas," Walter informs you. "She's taking classes at NYU and modeling on the side."

"You're in college?" you say. She looks thirteen years old, tops. Except for the boobs.

Carly casts her eyes down with false modesty. "I took accelerated classes back at home. I finished my high school equivalency in two years."

"Wow" is all you can think to say.

"She's actually taking a class with Handelman." You and Walter just finished reading his seminal book, *Leaving America*, in poli-sci. He's been checking the rest of Handelman's work out of Therot Library since and devouring it.

"I'm such a groupie," confesses Carly. "I had to petition to get into the class, since it's normally reserved for grad students, but it was so worth it. The man is beyond brilliant." She rests her hand on Walter's forearm. The girl is a full-on genetic freak—flawlessly beautiful and beyond-her-years intelligent. "You should totally come with me to hear him lecture. I'll sneak you in, no problem."

"Really? That would be amazing." The two of them exchange numbers in front of you as you pretend not to care. And why is that so hard to do? Walter's not your boyfriend, he's your friend, and you have absolutely no claim to him. Why shouldn't he chat up this paradigm of female perfection? What kind of friend would deny him that?

The jealous kind.

When they start discussing great late-night jazz clubs in walking distance, you see where the conversation is headed and put your foot down. "Um, Walter?" you interrupt, relishing Carly's annoyance. "Could I talk to you for just a minute?"

You are most likely to . . .

pull him aside and repeat what you overheard about Hunter. Maybe it's nothing . . . but you should let him decide that. Plus, let's be honest, it may stop his momentum with Carly. Continue to Snapshot #39 (page 189).

or

urge him to head back to campus . . . you're getting nervous about flouting so many rules. Yeah, that's it . . . the rules. Has nothing to do with Carly, right? Continue to Snapshot #40 (page 197).

Saturday, February 15, 9:55 p.m.
Pennyworth House

Oona recovers herself on Mr. Worth's front porch as you watch from a safe distance: after the briefest cry, she smoothed her hair, vigorously brushed away her tears, and marched into the night. The glimpse into her softer, more vulnerable side was closed, possibly forever. You'd done nothing, afraid of having her rage redirected your way. Was it the right decision? Well, hard to say. Not the bravest, but perhaps the safest.

Now you and Walter are back in your dorm room, cozied up in your usual *Casablanca*-watching spots: you on the couch with a blanket draped over you; Walter in his favorite chair, feet propped on the coffee table.

"Scrabble?" Walter suggests. The two of you have a running game. You nod and grab the board from the bookshelf, setting it up between you.

You and Walter both look up at the distant wail of fire truck sirens.

"Weird," Walter says. "That's a sound you don't hear much around here."

"Or ever." You pull a blanket around your shoulders. "Hope it's nothing serious." Oona pops back into your head. She may be a bully, but it's not like she'd actually do something to hurt Worth's Other Woman. Right?

Of course not. Don't be ridiculous.

The two of you refocus on your Scrabble game. "You almost closed the gap in our last game," Walter says, looking at the score sheet. He's always winning—it's just a matter of by how much. As he sets up the board and dispenses letters, you rummage around for a pen to keep tally, but can't find one in the box. So you head over to Spider's desk, opening her top drawer to find one.

Your hand grazes a stack of math exams, and you can't help but notice the grades on them. A. A+. A. That's odd. You and Spider are both taking pre-calc this year with Mr. Paluschka, and you know she's been struggling. You've spent several late nights trying to help her get up to speed. So you're surprised—if not a little shocked—to see she's doing so well. Why wouldn't she have told you?

Then you notice the names at the top of the exams—none of them are Spider's. They date back several years, too, but you recognize test questions from exams you've taken recently. Your stomach sinks. Could Spider be cheating? There's a strict honor code at Kings, and she certainly doesn't seem like the type to break it—but then again, you know she's been stressed about keeping her B– average, a requisite for keeping her athletic scholarship.

Not wanting to bring Walter into the drama, you quickly grab a pen, slam the drawer shut, and return to the common room couch. You'll have to get Spider alone tomorrow so you can ask her about what you found—hopefully, it's not what it looks like. Maybe there's a good explanation . . . you just can't think of what that might be.

"You're up first," says Walter.

After a few minutes, you come up with MANATEE. Not bad, you think. Not bad at all. "Beat that, Mr. Mensa," you tease.

Walter studies his board. He seems oddly nervous, as he plops the little squares onto the board. When you look down at what he's spelled out, you realize why. It's just three tiles. The middle one was blank, but Walter has drawn a small red heart on it.

I ♡ U.

Gulp.

Walter looks you in the eye. You feel kind of dizzy.

"Here's looking at you, kid," says Bogart in the background.

A Scrabble board confession. It's such a Walter way of copping to his feelings. Sweet, but admittedly dorky. But *sweet*! Before you can formulate a response, Walter leans forward and kisses you gently on the lips. Your first real kiss. And it feels just like you'd always hoped it would. Swept up in the moment, you kiss him back. But then your brain catches up to remind you that it's Walter, and crossing this line will change your friendship forever, and no matter how surprisingly good a kisser he is, shouldn't you really give this some thought?

Well . . . heart or head?

You are most likely to . . .

give in to the moment. Maybe it's Bogart, maybe it's Walter . . . but you're suddenly feeling romantic. Throw caution to the wind and see if this could spell L-O-V-E. Continue to Snapshot #41 (page 202).

or

think it through. The last thing you'd want to do is lead Walter on—it could destroy your friendship. Continue to Snapshot #42 (page 208).

SNAPSHOT #23

Saturday, February 15, 9:45 p.m.
Faculty Row

"Hey," you whisper tentatively as you approach Mr. Worth's porch. Dangerous as it feels, you can't walk away from someone who's hurting so much. Even when the someone is Oona. "You okay?"

In one efficient motion, she whips around to face you. You stop breathing. Her eyes are a little puffy and you can tell she's been crying, but her expression is fierce. You've made a mistake, approaching her when she's so vulnerable. Without turning, you start to edge backward. "Of course I am," she hisses.

You're past the point of no return. It's too late to creep away—Oona knows you've seen her cry, and she'll never forgive you for it. Might as well just say what's on your mind, as there's not much to lose now. You clear your throat. "Mr. Worth is a complete d-bag who didn't deserve a girl like you in the first place." The words spill out quickly. "In my opinion."

Oona just blinks. When she speaks again, you notice her voice has softened a bit—but only just a bit. "Do I know you?"

Oona pens a column called "Social Lives" for *The Griffin*, which means you've sat in about a dozen meetings with her. Often right across the table. Figures she barely remembers your face. "We work together on the newspaper. I'm a freshman."

"Right, now I know who you are." She taps her forehead. "You and Dearborn."

"What?" Your heart speeds up. There's no "you and Dearborn." There's only "Annabel and Dearborn." "You mean Henry?"

Oona snorts. "The goo-goo eyes are pretty nauseating. But isn't he, like, dating your roommate or something?"

Could she really be saying what you think she's saying? Is your crush on Henry that obvious? This girl doesn't miss a thing . . . except, apparently, when it comes to her own love life. "He is. We're just friends."

"Whatever. Something tells me you're not the leading authority on men."

You feel a flash of anger, and momentarily forget to whom you're speaking. "And you are?"

Oona blinks again. "My relationship with Martin was complex. Trust me, you could never understand." She's standing next to you now, squinting back toward his cottage. You're both silent for a few moments. "But you're not wrong that he's an asshole."

She starts walking briskly toward the Quad. You stay rooted in place until she looks over her shoulder at you and gestures impatiently for you to follow. "Well, come on. I hate drinking alone."

Yikes. You quickly text Walter so he's not worried about you.

But maybe he should be.

→ *You're in for it now. Head back to dragon's lair . . .*
Continue to Snapshot #23A (page 115).

SNAPSHOT #23A

Saturday, February 15, 10:23 p.m.
Merritt House

"How come you're not at Midwinter's? I would have guessed your little rooming group would have rushed right over," asks Oona in a bored voice, pouring herself another stiff martini. Her lavish single in Merritt House makes your professionally decorated suite look blah. Inspired by Old Hollywood, her room is pure glamour, from Art Deco wallpaper to the white fur draped casually on a velvet settee. You tell her the story of your night, more or less, and she waves her hand. "You're not missing anything. A bunch of kids getting wasted in the woods. It's uncivilized, frankly, but what can you expect?" Her phone has been buzzing with new text messages, and she finally deigns to look at them. Rolling her eyes, she sips her martini. "I'm not coming," she says aloud as she texts back.

"Are your friends giving you a hard time for not being at the party?" you ask. Maybe she should go, you think but don't dare suggest.

"My friends know better than to give me a hard time. But I'm missed, of course."

You crack a smile. "Of course."

"You're not drinking."

You glance at the vodka tonic in your glass and take an obligatory sip. Not bad. "So how long were you and Mr. Worth . . . together?"

She scowls. "Thanksgiving. I stayed on campus during break, sensing there was something going on between us." You involuntarily shudder, which she chooses to ignore. "Basically I didn't leave his house for four days. It was . . . magical." Magical? Not the adjective you would have chosen—but then again, not the guy you would've chosen.

"Thanksgiving . . . so that's a long time. Nearly three months?"

"It got serious quickly. We talked about traveling this summer to my mother's house in the South of France, since she's never there. For the past few weeks, he's been a little distant. I figured he was just busy. That's what he told me, anyway." Her face suddenly contorts with rage, transforming her stunning features into something terrifying. "It turns out he was getting busy with some piece-of-trash townie!" She's on her feet again, pacing around the room like a panther.

"I'm so sorry, that must have been so painful."

"Trust me, it'll be more painful for her. I saw them together this afternoon. She owns the bookstore." Oona gulps her martini again, intent on getting sloshed. "It's pathetic. How could he leave me for some 30-something bookworm loser? Heather

McPherson. That's her name. She probably, like, lives with her parents. It's *humiliating*."

You know exactly who Heather is. The name hadn't registered before, but the description makes it clear. She's the willowy blonde who lives and breathes books and always has the best recommendations. Over the past few months, the two of you have developed a loose friendship. Yes, she does live with her mother, who is quite ill and relies on her for nearly everything. The last thing Heather McPherson needs or deserves is Oona's wrath—or a lame boyfriend like Worth who's willing to sell her out to save his own ass. No doubt Worth never mentioned to Heather that he was surreptitiously seeing one of his students. And you see now that the crux of Oona's anger isn't Worth's betrayal . . . it's the incredible blow to her ego.

"Oona, listen," you say as calmly as possible. "You know that Worth didn't leave you for Heather, right?"

She's listening now—still pacing, but listening.

"I mean, come on. The guy's an almost middle-aged history teacher, and he finds himself in a hot affair with the most sought-after girl at Kings. A girl so out of his league in every single way, he has no choice but to hit the self-destruct button. You think Worth didn't know that you would tire of him in, like, two more weeks? That he was just a passing fancy for you? Meanwhile, he was setting himself to be completely destroyed when that moment inevitably came."

"You're right," Oona says. It's funny how you can almost see something releasing inside her. "No, you're absolutely right."

"Of course, it was weak and cowardly, sparing himself the future pain of your rejection by pretending to care about someone else. But can you really blame him?"

Oona settles into another chair and rests her drink on the table nearby. "I guess not. But still—"

"Still nothing. He couldn't handle you, and you know it." You quickly extinguish that spark of her anger. "You need a much, much stronger man than Martin Worth." This much, at least, is true. You can tell your little speech has taken the fire out of Oona's rage—and hopefully Heather is out of her line of fire.

"You know something?" Oona looks at you with something resembling respect in her eyes. "You're not stupid. Relative to the population of this lame-ass school, you're not stupid."

It's as close to a compliment as you're likely to get from Oona.

"Where are you from, doll? Some podunk town in Massachusetts, right? I remember it had a particularly depressing name."

What? A tiny bubble of panic explodes inside you. First Oona barely remembers your name, and now she knows where you grew up in Hope Falls? And that it's not the "bucolic countryside" you've painted it as to everyone else?

"Hope Falls," you say in a quiet voice. The confidence you'd felt just a moment ago, when you thought you'd dismantled Oona's rage and brokered a peace, is evaporating fast. Oona smirks at you, noting your discomfort with sociopathic pleasure. "How do you know that?"

"I make a habit of knowing," she says, taking a nonchalant sip of her drink. "Knowledge is power, doll. I have a friend in Admissions who lets me peek at the new admit applications. If I remember correctly, your mother"—she taps her forehead, the smile still on her face—"works at the local Shoprite? Good for you for getting here, I say. Humble beginnings, and all that."

"I should go," you say, standing up, feeling the blood rush to your cheeks. You wish your family's background didn't cause you discomfort, but it does. It's just easier to pretend your life in some way resembles the lives of your wealthy new friends. You don't want anyone feeling sorry for the scholarship kid. Why does anyone need to know that your mother has a minimum-wage job? That your parents could never afford to send you to a school like Kings? Why is it anyone's business?

You head for the door, regretting now that you ever tried to help Oona de Campos. Just when you thought you'd had a breakthrough with her, she'd made it clear that the two of you would never be friends. And now as you leave, she doesn't bother to say goodbye—instead waving you off with a flick of her hand as she crosses the room to refresh her drink.

The End

SNAPSHOT #24

Saturday, February 15, 9:15 p.m.
Lakeshore Woods

"Maybe I didn't make myself clear," Oona says slowly, her violet eyes narrowing on Hunter. "Leave before this gets ugly."

"It got ugly the moment you walked over," Hunter lashes back.

The situation is a nanosecond away from going nuclear—if you're going to intervene, it has to be now. "Oona, we're all just here to have fun. Walter's not bothering anyone."

"He's bothering me." Her hatred is suddenly laser-focused at you, and it's downright blood-chilling. "Stay out of this, freshman, unless you've got a death wish."

"Oona, chill." Crosby Wells puts a hand on her shoulder. You turn to find the scruffy, gorgeous senior standing so close you can smell his musky cologne. Finding it oddly calming—not to mention, sexy—you inhale as deeply as you can without being totally obvious. "It's okay. He'll stay for a beer or two and then hit the road. I'm vouching for him." Crosby pulls Oona away, whispering in her ear, calming her down—for the moment. He comes right back. "Sorry about her. Oona gets a little worked up sometimes. Anyway, I'm a huge fan of your work, Hunter. You were brilliant in *The Lost*."

You want to hug him. Is the showdown really over? They should send this guy to the Middle East! How did he appease Oona so quickly? Crosby was like . . . the Bitch Whisperer, or something.

He'd always kind of intrigued you. There's just something mysterious and cool about Crosby Wells. Libby told you that Crosby's father is some mega-powerful Wall Street hitter, but you'd never guess it from his son's thrift-store hipster clothes and laid-back demeanor. And anyway, he just saved you from a terrifying confrontation with Oona.

"Thanks so much," says Hunter. "Do you know these guys?" She quickly introduces you and Walter, and you feel a surge of excitement when Crosby looks you straight in the eyes and shakes your hand. His grip is strong, and you remember seeing him play guitar on the Quad last fall, watching his hands move deftly over the strings.

"Good for you, standing up for your friend," Crosby says. "That's gutsy. Most people find Oona intimidating, especially when she's angry. She and I grew up together in New York, so I get her, but I give you credit."

"Thanks. You're a musician, right?" you ask, *feeling* gutsy now. There's something exhilarating about knowing you stood up to Oona and lived to tell the tale. Besides, Crosby seems genuinely impressed.

"Yeah, I started a band last year with some friends." When

he talks, his dark hair falls in his eyes, and he pushes it back with one hand.

"What kind of music do you play?"

"It's sort of a hybrid of folk, rock, hip-hop, and soul." He smirks, as if hearing himself for the first time. "Everything, really, but opera. And hey, never say never."

You chat a little about music—about your favorite groups, and his, about some great shows you caught in Providence last summer—before you feel his hand touch down lightly, and briefly, on your arm. "We've got a show at the Spigot next weekend, if you're interested," he says. "My buddy bribed the bouncer to let in kids from Kings, as long as you have a decent ID. Anything should work."

A fake ID . . . You kick yourself for not getting one made when you visited Libby in New York City over Thanksgiving. She knew a guy who could make them, all you had to do was show up at his apartment—but at the time, you hadn't felt like dealing. It cost eighty bucks, which seemed steep. You'd been more interested in going to museums and checking out the UN. Idiot! You admit to Crosby that you're completely fake ID–less.

He scratches his chin. "Maybe my cousin could give you her old one. You look a little like her."

Who knew Crosby Wells was so nice? You thank him and tell him you wouldn't want to put him or his cousin to any trouble . . .

"No biggie, I'll ask. Then you'll have no excuse not to

come to our show." When Crosby takes you in with his dark, soulful eyes, you really do forget about Henry for a moment. This is good. This is progress—

And just like that, Henry appears next to you. Damn. "Have you seen Annabel?" he asks, not bothering to acknowledge Crosby. "One minute I was talking to Josh about newspaper stuff and she was next to me. And then she was gone. Now I can't find her anywhere."

That's pretty weird. You excuse yourself from Crosby and follow Henry around the party, both of you calling Annabel's name. No sign of her. Her phone is going straight to voice mail. At the outside edge of the clearing, you and Henry stop and look at each other. The woods are pitch-black. Hopefully she didn't venture too far on her own.

"Should we head back to campus to look for her?" The skin between Henry's gray eyes is pinched, the sure sign that he's worried. He stands with his back to the woods. "Unless you'd rather stay and talk to Crosby."

"Excuse me?" You step closer, sure that you misheard that last bit. Why would Henry sound jealous?

"Forget it," he says quickly, shaking his head as though to dislodge an unwanted thought. "I say we just go. We know she's not here. She's probably back at the dorm, and maybe she forgot to charge her phone." You look at each other. It doesn't sound at all like Annabel. "Tell Spider and Libby to keep an eye out for her and call my phone if she turns up."

You pause for a moment, not sure if being alone with

Henry is the best thing for you. It's hard enough being with him in a crowd. Maybe you'd be better off staying put, and hey, you wouldn't mind flirting some more with Crosby. But Henry's got you worried about Annabel, too. Why would she have just left, without telling anyone where she was going?

You are most likely to . . .

→ *set off with Henry to find your friend. What if Annabel's really in trouble? Continue to Snapshot #32 (page 160).*

or

→ *tell Henry you'll stay at the party and keep an eye out for her return. You're sure she's fine, and it's not a good idea for you to be alone with her boyfriend. Better to be alone with Crosby, who's actually available. Continue to Snapshot #9 (page 47).*

SNAPSHOT #25

Saturday, February 15, 9:34 p.m.
Lakeshore Woods

"Maybe I didn't make myself clear," Oona nearly growls, her violet eyes narrowing. "You need to leave. You need to leave now." There's a purple vein pulsing on her left temple, like her head might actually detonate if she doesn't get her way and fast.

"No problem," says Walter, reaching out for his cousin's arm. Hunter stays rooted in place. "We don't want any trouble."

But it's too late for that. The moment to avoid trouble, to diffuse the tension, is past. Now the fight is on. Hunter and Oona are practically sniffing each other, like alpha dogs competing for control of the pack. Who has the upper hand is a hard call: Oona looms over Hunter and looks physically stronger, but Hunter has a wild ferocity behind her eyes. Hunter is mega-famous with fans across the world, but Oona has a dictatorial presence at Kings and a ready army of fearful soldiers. As they circle each other, the crowd of frenzied onlookers grows around them. This is a heavyweight fight for sure.

You're jostled on all sides as kids jockey for a better view, making it hard to see. The moment in which you might have been able to throw yourself in the middle between these two girls has passed—now you're fully blocked in, unable to move. With an obstructed view, you witness what happens next as a series of disconnected snapshots. Oona seems to push Hunter, although it's possible that she herself has been pushed from behind by the enclosing crowd. Hunter loses her balance, lurches a few steps. She's way too close to the bonfire. There is a collective gasp, loud and horrible to your ears. The next thing you see are the flames licking off of Hunter's head as Walter yanks her through the mass of onlookers. *Hunter Mathieson is on fire.* Is this really happening? Walter somehow manages to part the waters, pulling her through the pack of gawkers. Not wasting a second, he grabs a wool blanket from an overturned log and throws it over her head. You can hear her muffled screams— but a moment later, when he pulls off the blanket, the fire is out. The crowd gasps again—is that all that they're good for?

Hunter's face is covered in soot and her auburn tresses have been singed nearly to the roots. She's sputtering with shock and outrage and terror. But she seems to be unharmed.

As Walter helps his cousin toward the path, you scramble to catch up, knowing that you belong next to them. You should have stood next to them before things escalated with

Oona. Maybe you could have done something, maybe not—but now you'll always feel guilty for staying silent.

➤ *Flip forward to Snapshot #25A (page 128) to see how the year turns out.*

SNAPSHOT #25A

Saturday, May 24, 11 a.m.
Hunter's Malibu Beach House

Three months have passed since Midwinter's Night. Not long enough to erase the haunting memory of Hunter's famous face engulfed in flames—or to forget that you did nothing to stop her fight with Oona.

But a lot has changed.

You and Walter are in Malibu. You landed this morning at LAX and headed straight for Hunter's seaside pad. It sounds like a dream getaway, but actually, it's stressful. Hunter gets out of rehab today—yes, rehab—she's due home any moment. Walter's there to support her on her first days home, and you're there to support him. To be the friend you should have been back in February, when Oona was bullying him.

"I still wish we could've picked her up," Walter says, pacing around his cousin's palatial living room. The poor guy is a ball of nerves. "I hate the thought of her just hopping in a car with a driver."

"I know. But Hunter thought that any scene outside the facility could draw paparazzi attention. Apparently they lurk outside just waiting for a glimpse of someone famous checking in or out of rehab."

"Right. I know you're right." Walter runs a hand through his hair. "Why anyone would want to be famous is beyond me." You're with him there. Even standing in Hunter's multimillion-dollar home, it just doesn't seem worth it.

As you learned back on Midwinter's Night, the pressures of fame had proved to be too much for Hunter and led her down a path of self-destruction. After her terrifying accident, she'd refused to go to the hospital. You and Walter had tried your best, concerned that she needed medical attention, but there was no convincing her. Then, back in his dorm room, you'd learned why: dissolving into tears, Hunter had admitted to a drug problem. Cocaine. She hadn't wanted to check in to the hospital because the doctors may have ordered blood work, and then found narcotics in her system, something she couldn't afford to have leaked to the press. Walter had been amazing that night—taking care of Hunter, reassuring her that everything would be okay—and ever since.

You hear a car in the driveway and Walter rushes to the window to see if it's Hunter. It is. He looks so nervous, making you appreciate yet again just how much he cares about his cousin and what a tremendous pillar of strength he's been for her. Walter had insisted on welcoming her home from her ninety days in rehab, and you'd been thrilled when he'd taken you up on the offer of some moral support. The ticket cost every last penny in your savings account, but it felt worth it. With your parents' permission, the school allowed you to leave campus for the weekend.

You'll fly back tomorrow morning—just when Hunter's parents are scheduled to arrive to spend some time with her. Hopefully, she'll get the support she needs to stay on track.

You're here as Walter's friend, but you've been harboring a secret since the night of the party. Seeing him take charge had cast him in a whole new light. He'd truly saved his cousin's life, a heroic act that's been followed by weeks of demonstrating just how caring and compassionate he is. You don't care if Walter is outside of the cool crowd at Kings. He's *above* the cool crowd—more mature, more true to himself, and frankly, more of a man than most of the popular guys.

You've kept your crush to yourself for now. Walter's had enough on his plate, to say the least, and you've wanted to be sure that your feelings were real. But they are. And they're only growing. In fact, they've grown so much that they've eclipsed the crush you used to have on Henry, who broke up with Annabel shortly after the Midwinter's party.

Tonight, after the two of you have helped Hunter ease back into her life a little, you'll tell Walter just how crazy about him you are. What will he say in return? You can't be sure. But every time you think about what might lie ahead, you can't help but smile.

The End

SNAPSHOT #26

Saturday, February 15, 9:23 p.m.
Lakeshore Woods

When you and Spider yank Libby away from Billy Grover, she's practically kicking and screaming. You'd known it wouldn't be easy. "What the hell are you guys doing?" she sputters once you're out of earshot.

"I'm pretty sure his friend put something in your drink," you whisper.

"What?" She gets so loud when she drinks. She's practically shouting at you, and you're less than three feet away.

"His friend may have slipped something in your drink."

"You're not serious." Libby stands with her hands on both hips, swaying back and forth a little. She hands you her drink. "Like a pill or something?"

You just nod. "I mean, I could be wrong. But I think that's what I saw."

Spider glances back toward Billy. "Libby, there's just something about that guy—we all think he's a little creepy. You could do a lot better, trust me. Like my friend Harry, from the guys' soccer team? He asked me the other day after practice if you were single."

"Which one is Harry?" Libby scans the crowd. Any thoughts of Billy seem to have instantly vanished from her head. Of all the reactions she could have had—fury at you for breaking her away from her crush; panic over the fact that said crush just potentially tried to *drug her*—this is one you'd never expected. "Ooh, is he the tall one over there?" When Spider nods, Libby begs for an introduction.

It makes no sense to you. Is Libby's ability to swing her romantic interest immediately to another guy the result of the alcohol? Or is she just wired differently than you? If only you could change directions on Henry so easily. What matters most to Libby is having a good time. She and Spider head over to meet cute Harry, leaving you alone with her potentially contaminated cup. You wonder what you should do with it. Turn it into Health Services for testing? Dump it on the grass? The very real possibility that Billy was going to hurt her—not to mention whether he might move on to do it to another girl—doesn't seem to weigh heavily on Libby's mind or conscience. But you're not sure that you can let Billy off the hook so easily.

It feels like time to go. Your thoughts have grown too heavy for a party. You slip away quietly, sending Spider a text once you're on your way home so the group won't be worried. On the way home, you're careful not to spill that drink. With each step, your conscience more clearly dictates what you have to do. You bring Libby's drink to Health Services, despite the fact that it's a hike to get there, you're freezing, and you'd rather be curled up under your duvet. Once there, the process is surprisingly straightforward. The doctor on duty doesn't seem to care about the party, or where the drink came from. Instead he fills out some forms and takes the drink from your hands, telling you he'll let you know results in the next few days.

When you finally get to lay your head down on your pillow, you expect to fall immediately to sleep. You're exhausted. But your thoughts race back to Henry and Annabel, and the wrenching feeling you'd had watching them embrace. Why did life have to be so complicated? Life wasn't perfect in Hope Falls—you were bored at school and had nothing to do on weekends—but at least it wasn't complicated. Or hard: your academic workload now is absolutely crushing at times, leaving you sleep-deprived and stressed. Or painful: heartbreak, disappointment, vulnerability all seemed to enter your life when you became a student at Kings Academy. The lows are lower, that's for sure. As you gradually drift toward sleep, you hope that one day the highs will be higher, too. You're overdue for some lofty highs.

The End

SNAPSHOT #27

Sunday, February 16, 9:45 a.m.
Pennyworth House

Naturally, you're the first one to wake up the next morning in Pennyworth 304—you beat your roommates home by a few hours last night. Annabel is passed out cold, her satin sleep mask over her eyes, and you can hear Spider's snore from the next bedroom. You dress quickly and slip out the door, grabbing *The Great Gatsby* to keep you company in the dining hall. As you walk down the front steps, the brisk air attacks every exposed inch of skin.

You're about to pull your hood around your ears and step up your pace when you're stopped dead in your tracks by what's in front of you. Someone is slumped on a bench in the small courtyard outside of Pennyworth. Stepping closer to get a better look, you gasp when you recognize Libby . . . passed out on a bench with her tights ripped, her hair in knots, her coat wide open . . . on one of the coldest mornings of the year.

You rush over and help her to her feet, immediately inhaling the strong alcohol fumes emanating from every pore, terrified by the pallor of her skin and her purple-blue lips. Her eyes flutter open ever so slightly—a prayer answered—as you clumsily get the door open and lug her up the stairs of Pennyworth, all the way to your dorm room. Banging on the door as you struggle to support Libby, you yell for Annabel and Spider, and they fall out of bed immediately to help. The three of you set to work, undressing the now shivering but conscious Libby, and then helping her down the hall to a warm shower. She vomits in the shower, which while gross comes as another relief—less booze in her system. You're not even thinking—you're just doing. The three of you wrap her in warm comforters and guide her back to her room. She's able to speak and says she can feel all her extremities, so you settle her into her bed and make her some tea on the illegal hot plate you keep in the common room. Annabel calls the local deli and asks them to deliver some egg and cheese sandwiches. Meanwhile, Libby drifts back to sleep.

It takes an hour before she's fully awake and able to talk. "What happened to you last night?" Spider asks, and every muscle in your body clenches. Because you know. The second you saw Libby, you knew. You should have trusted your instincts. You should have pulled her away from that horrible creep Billy the second you thought—or even vaguely suspected—something might have been put into her drink.

"I have no idea," Libby says, shaking her head. She groans a little. "I mean, obviously I had way too much to drink. I remember talking to Billy, but I honestly have no idea what happened after that. I must have blacked out."

"I feel like a schmuck. I should've been keeping an eye on you." Spider is visibly furious with herself. "I left early."

"You did?" That's weird. You could've sworn you heard Spider come in sometime around two, whack her shin on the fancy umbrella stand Libby insisted on keeping by the door, and swear loudly.

"I, um, went home with someone," Spider says, staring at the ground. "But that's between us, okay? I don't want everyone to know yet."

You and Annabel exchange glances. This is news. Spider's never expressed the slightest interest in romance before—and now she's hooking up with someone? You can tell Annabel's wondering the same thing: did Spider go home with a guy or a girl?

"Who is it?" Libby asks, her voice hoarse.

Spider takes a deep breath. "Dexter Trent. From the soccer team. You guys probably don't know him—"

"Are you kidding?" Annabel smiles. "He's in my Spanish class. That guy is awesome. Spider, I'm so happy for you."

"It's no big deal. Just between us, okay? You know the other girls on the team will be merciless if they catch wind. We're taking things slowly. But yeah, he's pretty great." She grins sheepishly. Mystery solved.

"Anyway, Lib, I'm sorry, too. I was completely preoccupied with Henry," says Annabel. "Actually, we broke up last night. I was in his room for hours. I'll give you the scoop later, I promise, but it was the right decision and I'll be okay. I'm just going to need some time before I can talk about it. I think I'm still in shock that it all unraveled so quickly."

You can't believe what you're hearing. All this went down while you were hoovering down cheese fries at the diner? Henry and Annabel were the perfect couple, and for as much as you've daydreamed of him being *your* boyfriend, the thought of them actually breaking up had never crossed your mind. There's a weird fluttery feeling in your stomach. You don't want to put a label on it because you're afraid to acknowledge that the feeling is excitement. Your body is having an involuntary reaction to the news that Henry Dearborn is single, no matter what it means for your best friend, making you feel like a horrible human being for the second time this morning.

"Did you and I hang out last night?" Libby asks, turning now to you. "Did you see what happened to me at the end of the night?"

The lump in your throat is now grapefruit-size. It's hard to breathe. You're afraid to tell Libby the truth about what you might have seen—but not telling her makes you an accomplice in whatever Billy might've done. "I ducked out early to go meet Walter. When I left, you were with Billy. I don't know, Lib, it's not like you to black out. Do you think he could have put something in your drink?" You haven't come clean, but maybe the suggestion is enough.

"I'm sure he wouldn't do that." Libby pulls the blankets up to her chin. "God, does my head hurt. This is the worst hangover of my life."

It strikes you that for a fifteen-year-old, Libby has endured more than her fair share of hangovers. You wish she'd slow down her drinking so that she could maintain better judgment. She seems too quick in letting Billy off the hook. What if he did something to hurt Libby during those blacked-out hours? Did he leave her to freeze out on that courtyard bench? And what if he tries to do this to another girl at the next party? He's innocent until proven guilty, of course, but that's all the more reason to get Libby to Health Services for some tests. "In any case, you should get checked out," you tell her, feeling grateful when Annabel nods her support. "We'll all go with you. I'm sure everything is fine, but you'll feel better knowing."

Libby's nose scrunches in distaste. "I'm not so sure about that."

"Please, Libby." You're willing to beg.

The three of you wear her down and she agrees to go. Once there, Libby's given a pregnancy test. An HIV test. A battery of STD tests, although the doctor tells her she'll need to come back to be retested, as some illnesses aren't immediately detectable. Suddenly the stress you felt during the midterm exams seems so minor and trivial in comparison to these tests that have life-changing consequences. The doctor gives her a full-body physical. Other than some weird bruises on her left arm, she seems okay.

But you're not. As you trudge home with your friends, you realize the full measure of the mistake you made last night. It'll be a few days before Libby gets some of her test results;

you won't be able to eat or sleep until she does. And even then you won't rest easy if she lets Billy off the hook. Who knows how many other girls may be hurt because you didn't blow the whistle?

Continue to Snapshot #27A (page 140).

Tuesday, April 8, 7:15 p.m.
Hamilton Dining Hall

"I've changed my mind," Libby says quietly. She's seated next to you in the dining hall as the rest of your group stands in the checkout line. "About Billy. I walked by him last night, you know, in the Quad, and he wouldn't even look at me. And it just pushed me over the edge. Why am I protecting this guy?"

"Libby, I'm proud of you."

"Well, I still have to run it by my parents. But yeah, I'm thinking I'm going to report what happened to Fredericks. I mean, the guy left me for dead on that freezing night. He's a complete scumbag. I don't love the idea of everyone knowing, but I can't let him get away with it."

Relief washes over you. For almost two months, you've had to accept Libby's decision to keep quiet about what happened—even after the lab results showed that she did have rophynol in her system that night. She was otherwise "lucky"—no STDs, or at least none that were immediately detectable, and no unwanted pregnancy. Still, you'll never forgive yourself for being so passive when a friend's well-being was on the line. You'd done your best to support her, but it's also been weighing on you that Billy and his friend were able to get away with what they did.

Annabel, flanked by Lila and Tommy, takes a seat. She looks at you and Libby. "What'd I miss?"

"Nothing," Libby says quickly. "Hey, did anyone take good notes in poli-sci today? I got stuck setting up chairs for the Senior Skits."

"Mine are decent," Tommy says.

And the dinner continues. Eventually, once her decision is final, Libby will fill in your other roommates on what she's doing. But for now, you feel honored that she's told you and proud of her for taking the harder path. It makes you even more determined that in the future, you'll do more to help a friend who might be in danger.

The End

SNAPSHOT #28

Sunday, February 16, 8:30 a.m.
Pennyworth House

When your eyes finally open the next morning, you immediately groan. It feels like you were hit, repeatedly, with a wrecking ball to the temples.

"I think she's up," you hear Libby whisper in the common room. The bedroom door opens and your roommates tiptoe in, Annabel clutching a greasy bag of takeout from Glory Days.

"Hey, buddy," says Spider in a whisper so uncharacteristically gentle it scares you. "We thought you could use some French toast. Well, Libby thought you'd prefer eggs and hash browns. So we got both. And OJ. And pancakes. Thought it might help you feel better."

A panicked feeling bubbles up inside you. Why are your roommates treating you with so much sympathy? Why does your head hurt *this much*? "What happened last night?" you ask. The last thing you remember is talking to Billy. Not really talking—just falling against him. The rest of the night is pure blackness, devoid of memory.

Annabel sits down on the side of your bed, as though it's

been decided that she'll be the one to break the bad news. "Sweetie, everything is okay. Thank God. Last night, we think one of Billy's friends slipped a roofie—or something like it—into your drink. Henry thought he saw it from across the crowd, but he's not sure. Anyway, he couldn't get to you before you took a few sips. Ten minutes later you started acting weird and falling a lot, like you were about to pass out. The three of us carried you home."

"You're heavier than you look, you know," Libby adds.

"A roofie—you mean, the date rape drug?"

"It's just a guess." Annabel nods.

Your head is spinning. Billy drugged you? Your friends—including Henry—carried your limp unconscious body home through the woods? No wonder you feel this awful. You shudder, unable to prevent yourself from thinking about what might have happened if Henry hadn't been paying attention. You look at Libby. If she's at all annoyed that you'd been sitting with her crush, she hides it well—all you can see on her face is genuine concern. It could have been her. It could have been any girl at the party.

"We've got to get you over to Health Services to be tested," Annabel says. "Rohpynol leaves the body after twenty-four hours. If Billy and his friends did this to you, they could do it to someone else."

You nod, wincing from the pain of such a small movement. Your tongue feels swollen and dry in your mouth.

Later, after you've had a few bites of food and let your

friends help you get dressed, it occurs to you that you should thank Henry. He was the hero in getting you out of a bad situation. "Do you think Henry's home?" you ask Annabel. "I should call him and thank him."

She and Libby look at each other. "I don't know," she answers.

"I'll call his cell. What's the number?" You pick up the landline phone, ready to dial, but Annabel remains silent.

"He knows you're grateful," Spider says. "You don't need to call right now."

Their strange expressions ignite a mini-panic in you. Did something happen with Henry last night? In your blacked-out state, did you profess your love—or otherwise humiliate yourself? "What's going on?" you ask, sitting down for the answer. "Why shouldn't I call him?"

"Of course you can call him. It's just"—Annabel looks weary, you notice for the first time, as though she's had a long night, too—"Henry and I broke up last night. I told him I thought we should make a clean break. He had brought up seeing other people, and I'd ignored it, pretending it was just a blip and everything would be fine. But last night, I realized I couldn't hold on to him if he wanted something else. I couldn't *convince* Henry to be with me. If he was having doubts, I needed to let him go. So I did. After all this happened."

"I can't believe it" is all you can manage to say, rubbing your temples. What does it mean? Annabel seems to be taking the breakup remarkably in stride, or maybe she's just putting on a brave face.

"It's insane," Libby says, throwing on a peacoat. "But I never thought he was good enough for Annabel, anyway." That's news, if it's true—but you appreciate Libby's loyalty. Annabel is going to need cheering up. She was the one to pull the plug on the relationship, but he was the one who'd put it on life support in the first place. You'd never seen it coming, and she probably hadn't, either.

"We should really get going," Spider says, helping you back on your feet.

It's hard to believe that so much could change in just one night. You'd thought Henry and Annabel would be together forever. You'd never worried that someone would try to hurt you, or that you would need to seek justice against them. The world isn't as safe as it felt a year ago, when you went to bed every night with your well-loved teddy bear and woke up to English muffins across a table from your parents.

Spider laces up your running sneakers, since it hurts too much to lower your head. "Ready?" she asks.

"Sure," you lie, and the four of you head out.

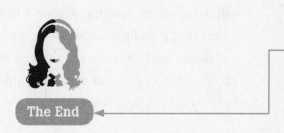

The End

SNAPSHOT #29

Saturday, February 15, 9:05 p.m.
Lakeshore Woods

Out of some combination of friendship preservation and self-preservation, you've stumbled away from Billy in search of a friend. The party swirls around you like an unstoppable kaleidoscope. The voices of the crowd, the throbbing music, the blindingly bright bonfire at the center of it all—overwhelm you. You've never been this drunk before. It's like you're caught in a riptide and unable to make it back to the safety of the shore.

When you feel a strong hand grip your arm and pull you toward a quieter spot, you follow without resistance, a rag doll. Only when you reach a tree stump outside the fray do you realize that the hand belongs to Oona de Campos. Even in your current state you know this is not good—that nothing good can come from being singled out by Oona—and yet your body still doesn't offer enough resistance when she pulls you to stand on the stump and plops something down on your head.

"Ladies and gentlemen," she bellows into a megaphone, silencing the crowd and deafening you. All eyes are now on her—or rather, you. "I give you the Freshman Mess!"

And before you can even make sense of what she's saying, your body is getting hosed down from several directions—with beer, you realize quickly, feeling it sting your eyes. The keg spigots have each been pointed at you by a senior jock. Billy Grover's manning one of the kegs, and seems to take particular glee in soaking you down to the skin. Your hair clings to both sides of your face, mascara runs down your cheeks. Your jaw drops open in protest. This cannot be happening. Your tormentors lift you off the stump and onto their shoulders, parading you around the party while chanting "FRESHMAN MESS! FRESHMAN MESS!" You can barely breathe, let alone absorb what's happening, but you do notice with horror that your miniskirt has somehow made its way closer to your waist, revealing your (also soaked) Hello Kitty underpants.

"Well . . . Hello Kitty!" Billy Grover sneers from below you, releasing another wave of cruel laughter from the crowd.

Finally, finally, your roommates negotiate your release, cover you with a blanket, and hustle you toward the path home. As you run, you happen to meet Henry's eyes. When he looks away quickly, embarrassed for you, it's the worst moment of the night.

→ *Sleep it off, Kitty. Maybe things will look brighter in the morning. Continue to Snapshot #29A (page 148).*

SNAPSHOT #29A

Tuesday, February 18, 7:05 p.m.
Pennyworth House

"This is absurd," says Spider, opening the door to find yet another stuffed Hello Kitty doll propped up against it in the hallway. "Get over it, people."

"It's harassment!" Annabel has been seething mad since the party. She keeps threatening to call her father's attorney, which, of course, is ridiculous—like you would sue Oona for humiliating you for being wasted (underage) at a party (after curfew) in the woods (off campus). You'd be expelled faster than she would! You and Libby stay silent, curled up on opposite sides of the common room couch. The four of you have been holed up since Saturday night, with the other girls venturing out to the dining hall periodically to stock up on provisions. It's just too much to walk through campus and hear the chorus of "Hello, Kitty" each time you pass by a group of upperclassmen.

The Freshman Mess. Not exactly the reputation you'd hoped to forge at Kings. "I'm never drinking again," you declare for, oh, the thousandth time.

"This will be old news fast," Annabel says, standing behind the couch and gently patting the top of your head. "Nobody will be talking about this by next weekend, sweetie, I promise."

You notice Libby arch one brow ever so slightly.

There's a short knock at the door, signaling the arrival of either Henry with bagels or Walter with notes from your American history class. You'll go to class again tomorrow, you've vowed to yourself—even though the thought of it makes your stomach clench with dread.

Spider opens the door and it's Henry. You haven't been able to look at him since the party, and he seems to feel similarly sheepish after witnessing your public humiliation. It's weird, but you feel like something between the two of you has changed. He kisses Annabel on the cheek. "Bagel delivery. Extra cream cheese, as requested."

"You're the best," says Libby from across the room. Not that she'd ever touch a carb-y bagel. She always hollows hers out with her fingers, scooping out the doughy good stuff so she's left with an empty shell. And she calls herself a New Yorker.

"Hang in there, kid," Henry says, addressing you for the first time as he heads for the door. "I'll see you in tomorrow's staff meeting, right? I have a few articles I'd like you to tackle for the next issue of *The Griffin*."

You exhale. The normalcy of his tone floods you with relief. Writing some articles—getting back into the rhythm of your life—is exactly what you need to do. After all, there's just one way for the Freshman Mess to redeem herself—so clean up your act and get back to work.

The End

SNAPSHOT #30

Friday, March 21, 4:30 p.m.
Pennyworth House

You watch Libby pack up the last of her boxes without saying a word. In fact, you haven't spoken to her all week—ever since she broke the news, via *e-mail*, that she'd be moving into a single for the remainder of the year. Even her devotion to Annabel wasn't enough to make up for the social disgrace of being *your* friend and roommate.

Apparently there are two honor codes at Kings. There's the linen-covered blue book you had to read and sign when you matriculated. And then there's the unspoken code: Thou shalt not, under any circumstances, rat out a fellow student. Or, God forbid, a party-full of fellow students. Ever since word got out that you'd spilled the beans to Fredericks, resulting in the party getting raided and dozens of students getting in trouble, you've been persona non grata at Kings. To say the least.

"You guys can keep the mini-fridge," Libby says, motioning for the movers to take the ikat-covered chair and the coffee table. Your common room is quickly becoming bare. Before long the only thing filling it will be tension.

"You're too kind," you mutter.

Annabel and Spider are both at sports—Spider healed in record time, thankfully, and Annabel is trying out for JV field hockey—and so you alone are there to witness Libby's ignominious defection. You just can't believe she'd gone so far as to request a freshman single in order to distance herself from you. There are just two and a half months left of school, so it's a hell of an effort just to make a statement. The statement is loud and clear and will be broadcast to the student body: Libby Monroe wants nothing to do with the campus pariah, either.

You're still getting creepy threats in your mailbox. Even Henry—who escaped and was able to clear a bunch of the crowd, thanks to a hastily dispatched text from Annabel warning him about the headmaster's raid—has been acting distant ever since the party.

At first Libby said little of your decision to come clean with Fredericks. But as the weeks went by, and it became clear that you would remain public enemy #1 at Kings, she'd grown colder. Two weeks ago, she'd started eating her meals with Tommy and Lila instead of her roommates. And now this. Her own room. Libby had made up some excuse about wanting more privacy to focus on her schoolwork, but you all knew her real reasons had more to do with social rank.

On the other hand, Annabel and Spider have been great, even when it's put them in the line of fire to defend you. They keep telling you that the whole thing will blow over soon, and

you hope they're right. Walter's been unflinchingly supportive, too. The two of you have been spending more time together than ever, so you're far from lonely. You wish you'd
begun Midwinter's Night being a better friend to him, rather
than bowing to Libby. If there's any silver lining to becoming
the least popular girl on campus, it's that from now on you'll
be able to recognize who your true friends are. You'd always
suspected Libby's true colors—the next time your instincts
point against someone, you'll pay more attention.

The End

SNAPSHOT #31

Thursday, March 6, 11:05 a.m.
Hemmingsworth Hall

You feel a trickle of icy sweat snake its way down the left side of your body. Standing next to you in the hallway, Spider, Annabel, and Libby are miserably nervous, too. None of you slept much last night. Instead, you'd numbed yourselves with a Kardashian marathon, trying in vain to forget the very real possibility that you could be expelled today. You're all scheduled to appear in front of the disciplinary committee, a stern-faced group of faculty and students, all sticklers for the rules.

You'd been the one to feed Fredericks a ridiculous excuse, claiming that you'd decided to do a late-night nature walk as a "roommate bonding experience." Your friends had all quickly echoed the story. But Fredericks didn't buy it for a hot second. He must have suspected that the Midwinter's party was under way and was just fishing for details about its location. In any case, he'd immediately called the dean of students to dispatch a troop of security guards and police officers into the woods. This was not his first rodeo.

The rest of that night had been a horrible blur. The only bright spot was Spider's prognosis—she'd been immediately whisked off to the hospital, where she was told she'd make a full recovery after just a few weeks of rest. Meanwhile, you, Libby, and Annabel were kept in custody at Fredericks's house, guarded across the kitchen table by his grouchy wife, until the phone rang with news that the party had been busted. Then the three of you were sent home, too late to tip anybody off to the raid. Except for that one text that Annabel managed to get off to Henry, thank goodness.

Most of the busted partygoers ended up being let off the hook. There were just too many transgressions for the school to exert its usual disciplinary rigor: half the senior class would have been at risk of losing their college placements. Instead, many were put on probation, and then subjected to a seem-ingly endless lecture by Fredericks in the school assembly hall. Slap on the wrist stuff.

But you'd lied to the man's face, and your roommates backed you right up. You can't expect to be treated with the same leniency. Today you'll find out.

The heavy oak door finally creaks open and Mrs. Morris, the school guidance counselor, wordlessly motions for the four of you to enter. Inside the room, the disciplinary committee—composed of four faculty members, two seniors, and two juniors—sit around a long oval table. They all look somber—make that morbid—as they read through a file on your case. Beads of sweat pop out on Spider's upper lip.

The facts of the case are presented concisely by Mrs. Morris: caught in the woods on the night of the party, you were untruthful to the headmaster when questioned about your reasons for breaking curfew. It's dishearteningly straightforward: you screwed up. Each person at the table weighs in with their disappointment over your choices. This does not look good. Finally, you're each given the opportunity to speak on your own behalf.

Annabel's face is buried in her hands. Spider has been crying since the opening remarks, ripping through the box of Kleenex one of the juniors at the table passed her way. You can't seem to come up with the right words to defend yourself, either. Before you can make the situation worse by saying the wrong thing, Libby clears her throat to speak.

"Members of the committee," she says, her voice surprisingly steady with poise and confidence. "It's true that my roommates and I were in violation of curfew on the evening in question. For that, we all sincerely apologize. We realize that this school has rules for a reason and by not adhering to them, we were not acting in a manner worthy of a Kings student." As you glance around the table, it's clear that you're not the only one impressed by Libby's authoritative tone. This is a side of her you've never seen before. "But we did not lie to Headmaster Fredericks. Was it a good idea to take a walk in the woods without letting anyone know? Clearly not. Our friend was injured, and we could have put ourselves in real danger. But we were not at the party. We were never at the party. You can ask anyone who *was* there. To my knowledge, that party is exclusively reserved for upperclassmen."

You start to see where Libby's going with this. You never showed up. How can they prove your intention to go?

"Maybe you didn't make it there, but come on. The party was where you were *headed*," a senior girl objects. You instantly and irrevocably despise her.

"With all due respect, that's not true." Libby says this with such unblinking conviction, for a moment you believe her yourself. You hope the committee is swayed, too. "My mother is a proud alumna of this school, as was my grandmother. Both of them have told me stories about winter walks through the woods with their closest friends. They made the same stupid mistake, you see—I was simply hoping to honor a tradition and cherished memory handed down by the women in my family."

Fredericks frowns, as if trying to decide whether Libby is completely or only mostly making this up. Mrs. Morris asks you to step outside while they deliberate.

In the hallway, nobody dares say a word for the next twenty minutes. If Libby's Hail Mary works, you'll thank her later. Mrs. Morris reemerges and you're brought inside again, all four of you barely breathing.

Fredericks is standing now up at the opposite head of the table. "I think it's clear that none of us are at all pleased with the choices your group made on the night of February 15. You flouted the rules, sneaking out from your dorm room and putting yourselves in real danger." He goes on like this for several more minutes, as your hands clench the arms of your chair with white knuckles. This is torture. "As a result, the committee has elected to punish you by prohibiting you from leaving campus for the remainder of the term. In addition, you will all attend study hall every Saturday morning, prior to your sports commitments. Last, you are all on probation. Any further violation of the rules of our school will *not* be met with clemency, I can assure you of that."

Spider lets out a loud exhale.

"And, Miss Monroe. Should your ancestors pass along any other traditions that are in violation of our established code of conduct, you would be wise to ignore them."

Libby nods vehemently. Fredericks's words are sinking in: you've gotten away with it this time. No expulsion. No suspension, even. Just study hall? After you profusely thank the committee and flee the room, the four of you clutch each other in a hallway hug. "Let's get out of here," you whisper, and you practically run back to Pennyworth, feeling so light you could fly.

"My dad was probably right," Annabel says once you're out of anyone's earshot.

"About what?"

"Oh, he wanted to have his lawyer call Fredericks. I begged him not to get involved, but he persisted. Maybe it helped?"

"My dad's attorneys called, too," Libby admits with a shrug. "They helped with that 'family tradition' story, too."

"Pretty genius, Lib. I couldn't keep Coach Clements away,"

says Spider, smiling. "You know what a bulldog she can be. Maybe she wore Fredericks down a little, too."

You don't say anything. Nobody had jumped to your defense. On the contrary, your parents had been livid with you when you'd told them what happened. A strange lump forms in your throat—which is ridiculous, given how lucky you just got. You could have lost everything and been sent home to Hope Falls High School with your head hung in disgrace. You should be feeling grateful and happy right now. Look at your roommates—their arms are draped over your shoulders like you've all just won the big game. This should be a moment of celebration.

Instead, you feel alone and powerless. Like a nobody. This time around, you benefited from your friends' powerful connections and allies. Next time, you might not be so lucky.

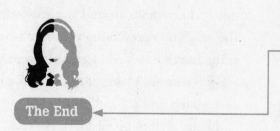

The End

SNAPSHOT #32

Saturday, February 15, 9:35 p.m.
Lakeshore Woods

"Annabel!" you shout into the woods. Now you're starting to get scared. Where is she? Why would she have rushed off without telling anyone? You and Henry have been walking through the woods for fifteen minutes. You just called Spider, back at the bonfire, and Annabel still hadn't turned up there, either.

Henry holds up the lantern so you can see where you're going. The woods around you are dark and still, and frankly, the only thing preventing you from being completely terrified is the fact that he's five feet away from you.

"I'm sure she's back at the dorm," you say out loud to reassure Henry and yourself.

Henry shakes his head. "I hope so." When he reaches for your hand to help you down a rocky section, you take it gratefully—your footing feels precarious. His hand is warm and dry despite the chill in the air, and you wish he'd keep it wrapped around yours. But that would be weird, so you gently pull yours away. "Did she tell you about last night?" he asks, caution in his voice.

Last night. The words feel loaded. They could mean so many things you don't want them to mean. A few weeks ago, Annabel had mentioned that she was starting to feel ready to go all the way with Henry. She was thinking about going on the pill. It'd be the first time for both of them. You'd managed to quickly change the topic whenever she brought it up. *Last night.* He's not going to tell you about something super intimate like *that*, is he? "Nope," you say, wishing you could come up with something—anything—else to talk about. Your mind is infuriatingly blank.

"Oh. I just think she might have been upset." Henry clears his throat. "We got to talking about the future. You know, whether it made sense to see other people."

Your jaw drops in shock. Annabel and Henry, the golden couple—seeing other people? Instinctively you know that Annabel would never, ever want to be with anyone but Henry. She's completely in love. She's named their future children (Daisy, Sadie, and Henry, Jr.). One thing was for sure: Henry had been the one driving the "see other people" conversation, and he was the one who felt unsure about their relationship. Your best friend must be devastated. Despite the fact that you've been secretly lusting after the guy for months, you feel nothing but sadness for Annabel right now. Why hadn't she said anything to you?

"I never meant to hurt her," Henry says, the anguish plain in his voice. "I'll never forgive myself if something were to happen to her."

You believe him. But you can also hear what he's not

saying—it's exactly what Annabel must have heard last night, and what she's been trying to deny ever since. Henry loves her, but he doesn't love her *enough*.

"Annabel!" you scream into the silent woods. You need to find her. You can only imagine the pain she's in right now. You walk faster, creating a little distance between you and Henry. Your head is swarming with uninvited thoughts. First he acts jealous over your mini-flirtation with Crosby, then he drops the bombshell that things are cooling between him and Annabel . . . could Henry possibly be interested in you? Bottom line, you need to not be near him. You need to not inhale his soap-coffee-woodsy-sexy smell. You need to crush the crush.

If you can.

Scaling over a small hill, your feet slip on some loose pebbles and you hit the ground. Before you can right yourself, Henry's caught up. He offers you his hand.

You are most likely to . . .

take it. Just because your heart is thumping a mile a minute doesn't mean he's feeling it, too. He's just helping you up, nothing more. Continue to Snapshot #33 (page 163).

or

mumble "I'm okay" and stand up by yourself. Your best friend is brokenhearted. Allowing any contact with Henry would make you feel vile. Continue to Snapshot #34 (page 167).

SNAPSHOT #33

Saturday, February 15, 9:35 p.m.
Lakeshore Woods

You slip your hand into Henry's, trying to ignore the electric current that seems to pass through you at his touch, and he pulls you to your feet. Your bodies are just inches apart now. The moon shines through the treetops.

"I need to tell you something," he says in a low voice, still clasping your hand.

Your heart is pounding. Inside your head, you're completely torn. Part of you is begging him to stop talking. To not say anything that will make this harder, or more confusing. But you remain silent. Because another part of you wants desperately to hear what he has to say.

"I told Annabel I wanted to see other people. But I'm just thinking about one person. I have been for weeks."

"Henry, don't." Your better self finally gets the words out. You know he's talking about you now, and you want nothing more than to kiss him—to be his girlfriend—to spend every minute you can with him. But it's so much more complicated than that. Better to just keep walking. Keep your focus on Annabel.

"We would wait. You know, if you felt the same. We would wait as long as it takes for Annabel to fully move on, which I know she will in time. I don't want to see her hurt, either." Henry laces his fingers through yours. "What do you think?"

Swirling with emotion, you take a small step back. "I don't know. This is a lot to take in." When you look at Henry with pleading eyes, he does the thing you most and least want him to do: he kisses you. Your first kiss. It's soft, gentle, just a promise of what could be.

Something flashes in the woods behind you. A camera.

By the time you hear the rustle of leaves, the shifting of pebbles underfoot, it's too late. Oona de Campos has her iPhone up in the air, and she practically cackles when she looks at the photo on her screen. "My, my!" she laughs, linking arms with you and Henry on either side.

"It's not what you think," you say—the timeworn words of those caught doing something extremely wrong.

"Oh, please." Oona just laughs. She shows you the picture: your lips are pressed up against Henry's. Incriminating evidence, for sure.

"Delete the photo," says Henry. "It'll only hurt Annabel."

"Maybe you should have thought of that before you decided to suck face with her best friend." Oona lets out a devious giggle. "But don't worry. I've got an idea for how we can work together. Annabel never needs to know."

"Work together?" Henry repeats.

This sounds bad. This sounds very, very bad. This sounds like blackmail.

"You guys are both whiz kids," Oona says. "I could use a little . . . *tutoring*. My parents are riding my ass about my GPA last semester."

Tutoring? You'll have to find the time, but tutoring doesn't sound like such a big deal. You look over at Henry. He doesn't look relieved.

"What kind of tutoring do you need?" he asks in a clipped voice.

Oona tips her head as you continue down the path, arm in arm. "I don't know. Like, that French paper we're supposed to write about *François le Champi*? I haven't had a chance to read the book yet. So maybe you could start with that. You know, just write a few pages. Then I'll look it over and make sure I understand it."

"You expect us to write your papers for you?" you ask, voice shaking a little.

"Well, yeah. It would be a huge help."

Henry stops in his tracks and pulls his arm away from her. "That's not tutoring, Oona. That's cheating."

Oona smiles brightly. "Is it? Well, I guess you're the expert."

You are most likely to . . .

capitulate. So you'll help her write a few papers.
It's either that or lose your best friend. Continue to
Snapshot #35 (page 171).

or

refuse to be bullied. You'll just have to tell Annabel
the truth, and deal with the consequences.
Continue to Snapshot #36 (page 174).

SNAPSHOT #34

Saturday, February 15, 9:55 p.m.
Glory Days Diner

Your phone pings with a new text message just as you're walking through the door to Glory Days, the old-school chimes over the door announcing your arrival. Walter looks up from his usual booth, and his face lights up when he sees you. You grin back. You may not have love in your life at the moment, but at least you have a great friend like Walter. And cheese fries on a cold winter night. It's not bad at all. You pause before heading toward him to read your new text, praying it's from Annabel, and find one from Henry.

> Annabel's fine. Back in your dorm room
> with her now. Would you mind giving us
> privacy for a little while? Thanks, H.

You can't help it: your stomach sinks a little. How terrible is that? You chastise yourself for not being more loyal to Annabel, but you can't seem to control feeling disappointed. Clearly what you'd felt in the woods—the tension between you and

Henry—was in your head. You try to push thoughts of Henry and Annabel's make-up session out of your head as you slide into the booth next to Walter. "How'd you beat me back here?"

"We left right after you and Henry did. Helen—Hunter—*Helen* decided she wanted to head to New York for a work thing."

"Oona was a bit much for her to take?" You swipe a fry off his plate, knowing he won't mind.

"I don't know. To tell you the truth, I'm a little worried about her. She didn't seem like herself tonight. It sounds like she's under a ton of stress from her management team. I don't know how she's coping." Walter sees the waitress and gestures for another root beer. "Anyway, did you find Annabel?"

"Apparently Henry just did. I don't know what happened yet, but she's fine. Safe and sound at home."

Walter looks at you intently, as if trying to decide whether to say what he's thinking. "You want my guess? She noticed the way Henry was looking at you tonight and got jealous."

It's such a un-Walter-like observation that you're caught off guard. Could it be true? You flash back to that feeling you had in the woods. It still seems far-fetched—especially as Henry and Annabel enjoy their "privacy" back in Pennyworth 304—but perhaps not outside the realm of possibility.

Walter leans forward. "Could you feel the same way about Henry? I mean, if he wasn't dating Annabel?" Something about his serious expression gives him away. You've always suspected that Walter might have a little crush on you, but now it's written across his face. Before you can answer his question, your phone pings again, this time with a text from Annabel.

> Henry just left. We're over. Could really
> use some company . . . and some double
> choc ice cream. Pick up, please? xo

"They broke up," you whisper to Walter, shocked by the way this night has unfolded. "I can't believe it. They were perfect."

"Apparently not," he says a little curtly. "So Henry is single."

You give him a pointed look. "Henry is completely off-limits. I'm worried about Annabel. She must be really upset right now."

"Of course," Walter says. "I know you are. She's lucky to have you as a friend." He slides over his cheese fries. "And so am I. Really, I hope you know how much our friendship means to me."

"I feel the same," you answer, reaching out to take his hand. Your heart aches when you see the sadness behind his smile. Why can't love be simpler? Why can't you take your feelings for Henry and transfer them to Walter?

"Should we head out?" he asks.

You nod, waving down the waitress. "I'll take a pint of double chocolate ice cream to go, please—and the check."

The two of you settle up and head back to campus, the conversation slow as you walk along through the lightly falling snow. Finally, when it's time to part ways, Walter gives you a hug. "Tell Annabel to hang in there."

"I will," you say, kissing his cheek goodbye.

The End

SNAPSHOT #35

Thursday, April 10, 1:15 p.m.
Morgan Lecture Hall

Very discreetly, you extend your right index finger—of which the fingernail has been relentlessly gnawed—and tap the laminate desktop. One tap means A. Two, B. Three, C. No taps at all tells Oona to scratch in the D bubble with her pencil. You glance at your nail. It looks even worse than it feels: raw, red, bloody around the edges from constant attack.

You can hear Oona scratching away with her number 2 pencil. You've moved past loathing her. At first, you'd wanted to lunge across the library table and strangle her each time she breezed in and slipped you an assignment—usually due the next day. Apparently Oona even procrastinated in having *other people* do her work. Two months later, what you feel now is far worse: dull resignation to the Faustian bargain you've made. Weary acceptance that you will be crushed with a double workload for the foreseeable future, unless Oona's parents decide to pull her out of school, or one of her creepy older boyfriends makes her his child bride.

Mrs. Harriman, the ancient proctor at the front of the

room, doesn't look up from her magazine. There's an honor code at Kings, and quite honestly, nobody would suspect you of cheating. You're seen as one of the good kids. Hardworking, honest. Of course, you know better.

And so does Henry. He's seated at the back of the room, hunched over his exam paper. You haven't spoken to him much since Midwinter's Night, but it's plain to see the toll the past weeks have had—clearly Oona's using him, too. Henry has dark circles under his eyes and his skin looks sallow. Somehow he's still managing to be incredibly hot—but something has changed between you, and even in the way you think about him. Maybe it's Oona, or maybe it's just your guilt over allowing that kiss to happen behind Annabel's back, but Henry feels like someone to avoid. Since his split with Annabel, he's been holed up in the newspaper office constantly—leading you to quit the staff. The last thing you want right now is to work hand in hand with Henry on an article. Hand in hand is what caused the problem in the first place.

You extend your index finger again, and tap three times. The answer to question 28 is C. Metabolic waste. You tap two times for question 29, and Oona immediately sprawls over her paper to fill it in. There's some poetic justice to it, perhaps. Caught cheating with your best friend's boyfriend, you're forced to do penance by cheating for Oona for the rest of the year. Maybe beyond. You can't think about when the blackmail will end—it brings on those splintering headaches that keep you awake at night, listening to Annabel's quiet exhales from the bottom bunk.

Maybe life would be easier if you just gave up on Kings and moved back home. Your public high school wasn't great, but it wasn't torture either. Some of the teachers may have been ho-hum, but at least you weren't facing a stress level that made your hair fall out, clogging up the drain in the shower. But of course, you'd be leaving Annabel and all your friends, giving up the incredible opportunities that come with a Kings diploma. Which is why you're still here. Which is why you're tapping the table once for question 30.

When Mrs. Harriman startles you by yelling that the exam is over, you put your pencil down and feel a momentary relief that you don't have to feed any more answers to Oona. Not that it's over. Deep down you know that it's far from over.

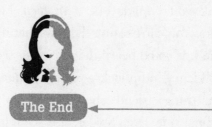

The End

SNAPSHOT #36

Friday, March 28, 1:40 p.m.
Hamilton Dining Hall

You spot Annabel in line for the bagel slicer and freeze, just as you do every time she comes into view. It's been impossible to avoid your former best friend, of course, just as it's impossible to avoid Libby, Tommy, or Lila, who strut past you on the Quad without so much as a passing glance. Libby, the leader of the pack, even had a "Team Annabel" T custom-made for herself. Their animosity toward you is so intense, one might think you'd made out with *their* boyfriends behind *their* backs. You can't blame them for hating you, though. Not remotely. If you'd heard the story—or seen Oona's photo of you and Henry in lip-lock—you'd be equally appalled. There are some things friends should never do. And you violated the cardinal rule. Even Spider can't seem to get over it.

Your roommates unanimously requested that you be removed from the suite and exiled to a single, which the school granted, so now you're living on your own. Spider had struggled with the decision, but ultimately sided with Annabel. It actually had come as a relief, leaving the horrible tension and stony silences of that room. And it's given you and Henry some privacy. Your new room is tiny, but the RA on your new floor is very lax, which means he can come over to study every night. Some nights he's even slept over, the two of you curled up together in your narrow twin bed. The more time you spend together, the more time you want to spend. Sometimes it's scary, feeling so head over heels in love, feeling so vulnerable. After all, just a few months ago, Annabel felt the same way. But Henry seems to return your feelings. In fact, he's even asked you to visit his family's beach house on Cape Cod this summer.

You take a seat at the end of a long, empty table with your soup and salad, wishing you had one of those Harry Potter invisibility cloaks for moments like these. Shoveling down your food as quickly as you can, you see Annabel squeeze into a seat at a table a few rows over, surrounded by friends. Judging by appearances, she's picked up and moved on with her life. Of course, you can never tell what's really going on beneath the surface. You know you caused your best friend genuine pain. It's hard to think about, but sometimes you force yourself to—Annabel crying, a box of tissues next to her on the couch in the common room, trying to make sense of her best friend and boyfriend abandoning her at once. It makes you feel like a heartless bitch, envisioning that scene—and is it possible that you are? You did, after all, steal the poor girl's boyfriend.

You pick up your empty plate and bowl and head toward

the conveyor belt that whisks them to a back room full of dishwashers. It's hard to enjoy rushed, lonely meals like this one. Your hunger was satisfied, but you don't feel full.

Someday, odds are that someone—maybe even Henry—will break your heart, too. And now you'll deserve it just a little.

The End

SNAPSHOT #37

Sunday, February 16, 12:07 a.m.
Oberon

The second kiss surprises you almost as much as the first. It sets off this crazy feeling inside you, not unlike the one at first sight of the New York skyline during the plane's descent. It's so good, in fact, that any doubts you had drop from your mind. You're kissing a guy you love spending time with. He's adorable. He's smart. He's sweet. So he's not the coolest. So he wears the same outfit every single day. So Libby will give you a hard time. So what?

"Get a room, you two!" Hunter says, coming up next to you. You can feel your face turn scarlet, but thankfully the club's way too dark for anyone to notice. Walter reaches for your hand. "Guess who might be starring in Scorcese's next film!" Hunter says. She's talking super fast and doing some weird thing with her jaw, like she's grinding her teeth together. Maybe it's overexcitement about meeting the legendary director . . . and possibly landing a role in his next project. But you suspect it might be something more than that. Could Hunter be using drugs?

"Wow, Hel, that's amazing. Tell us everything," Walter says, still holding your hand. You wonder if he's noticed anything strange in his cousin's behavior. He does seem to be watching her closely.

As Hunter fills you in, still talking a mile a minute, you try to listen but you're still reeling from what's just happened with Walter. There's a lot to process. Could a romance with your best bud actually work? In some ways, it seems perfect. But it's a little scary, too. If it doesn't work, you're down a seriously important friendship.

"What do you think, should we head back to campus?" Walter asks, interrupting your thoughts.

"The plane's ready whenever you guys are," Hunter says. "I'll call the pilot. I think I'll spend the night here, though." She's rubbing her arms like she's locked in a subarctic meat locker, when in fact the club is steamy warm.

"Do you want my sweater?" you ask.

"What? No, no, I'm fine."

After saying your goodbyes, you and Walter step outside to find paparazzi waiting for their last feed of the night. You walk quickly to the car, but of course the photogs take no interest in a couple of nobodies. Still, you love the feel of Walter's hand on the small of your back as he protectively hurries you toward the open car door. How could so much change between you so quickly? You'd literally never entertained any thought of Walter as a romantic prospect—and now the touch of his hand gives you goose bumps.

Just then the door of the club swings open again, and Hunter—looking a little bit disheveled—teeters out a few steps. The cameras come to life. "Walter!" she calls out. The two of you hustle back toward her. "Listen, don't tell my folks about tonight, okay? They hate that I go to clubs, or whatever. Between us, okay?"

She seems really out of it. There's no denying there's something going on with her. Walter gives her a kiss on the cheek. "I'll call you tomorrow, Hel." Obviously he shares your concern, but now—in front of a dozen greedy photogs—is not the moment for any kind of confrontation. Whirling around, Hunter hurries inside the club and the two of you head homeward—a place you suddenly want to be very badly.

To read about what lies ahead for you, Walter, and Hunter, continue to Snapshot #37A (page 180).

SNAPSHOT #37A

Sunday, February 16, 10:05 a.m.
Glory Days

"You're being way too cagey," Libby says, shoving aside her barely nibbled stack of buttermilk pancakes to rest both elbows on the table. "You didn't come home till after two. Start talking, lady."

Your roommates are usually the ones with the good scoop, the juicy headlines, so it feels pretty fun knowing that you're about to drop the mother lode on them. Meeting Hunter—Walter's cousin. Flying to New York. Kissing Walter. You don't know how they—well, Libby—will react to that last news item, but you've decided to pretend you don't care. Maybe someday soon you won't.

You open your mouth to speak, but before you can say a word, Libby's phone buzzes with a fresh e-mail. She glances at the screen and her eyes grow as wide as Glory Days' jumbo platters. Staring at you in utter disbelief, Libby wordlessly hands her phone to Annabel, who claps a hand over her mouth. Then she looks at you. Oh boy. You grab for the phone, but Spider beats you to it.

"Were you with *Hunter Mathieson* last night?" Spider practically screams, causing every head in the diner to whip toward your table.

Now you've officially stopped breathing. Libby's phone has finally made its way to your hands and you stare in horror at a photo of you, Walter, and Hunter outside of Oberon last night. "Where did that photo come from?" you ask Libby frantically. Broken curfew. Off campus. Underage at a club. This is all so, so, so bad. Expulsion-bad.

"Someone forwarded it to me. Hang on." Libby scrolls back, shaking her head. "It looks like it's going around the school. Some celebrity blog must have posted it this morning. Do you realize how cool this is?"

"Do you realize how dead I am?"

"Maybe it won't make its way to Fredericks," Annabel says, but you can see that she's inwardly freaking out, too.

"Or *any* of the faculty?" Your life is over. And Walter's. All the happiness you'd felt when you woke up is gone.

"Tell us everything," Libby insists, still focused on celebrity gossip rather than your imminent expulsion. You see clearly how little she cares about you. "How did you meet her? Don't leave out the tiniest detail." She stabs a pancake from her abandoned stack and slathers it with butter. "Only then will I forgive you for not calling and inviting us with you."

Before you can say a word, Walter bursts through the doors of the diner. He seems so upset you don't even have time to react to seeing him for the first time since he dropped you off at your door with a goodnight kiss. "Did you see the photo?" he whispers once he gets to your booth.

"Just did."

"I just got a call from Fredericks. He wants us both in his office in an hour."

"You're kidding me." You can't breathe. Expulsion seems inevitable. Flying to New York after curfew without any permission? Not even your roommates had known your plans. It was reckless—stupid, really. Why didn't you think it through more?

"Listen, I'm taking full responsibility for this," Walter says. "I forced you to go with me. There's no reason for both of us to get kicked out."

Wow. He's an even better guy than you'd realized. But there's no way you're letting him take the fall.

"Forget it," you tell him. "We're in this together. But I might have an idea."

It's a long shot, but it's all you've got.

Will you get a second chance or be sent packing? Find out by continuing to Snapshot #37AA (page 183).

SNAPSHOT #37AA

Sunday, February 16, 11:15 a.m.
Headmaster Fredericks's office

"So let me get this straight," Fredericks says, pushing back his chair and striding around his enormous mahogany desk to lean against the front of it. "The two of you broke curfew, flew to Manhattan without any permission from the school or your parents, all in order to confront Hunter Mathieson—who is Walter's cousin—about her drug addiction. So that you could help her get clean, and persuade her to cooperate in an anti-drug campaign that will be produced by our Student Council and posted online?" Fredericks looks like he's had a long night, too, which he has—you heard from your room-mates that he managed to bust the Midwinter's party as it was winding down, snagging at least four graduating seniors before they could escape through the woods. Usually Fredericks is immaculately groomed, but this morning he's sporting sil-ver stubble and wearing his slippers. It makes him seem only slightly less terrifying.

"Sir, it was a mistake," Walter begins, following the script the two of you had rehearsed all the way from the diner . . . between desperate phone calls to Hunter.

"But it was a mistake made with the intention of helping the school," you add. You explain that once Hunter is finished with rehab, she's committed to narrating a series of short anti-drug films. She'll use her high-profile connections to Hollywood directors and filmmakers to ensure the quality of the films. All in all, it's a huge victory for Kings and for the mission of your anti-drug committee . . . exactly the coup that you and Walter, as co-chairs of the committee, had hoped to score.

Once you've finished, you sit back a little, trying to gauge whether Fredericks has bought your story. He rubs his brow. "I can't let you off the hook for breaking curfew. The rules are not meant to be broken, you know, and you could have put yourselves in danger."

Despite his stern tone, you feel a ray of hope.

"But you've both been exemplary students. And these films do sound worthwhile. Study hall for both of you every Saturday through the remainder of the year."

Yessssssssss!

You feel like launching into the Hallelujah Chorus, and can tell that Walter does, too. Study hall? Study hall means you'll still be here!

"And I want full approval, of course, over the project. Nothing goes out until I've had a chance to look at it, and give my comments."

"Of course, sir," Walter says.

"A campaign like the one you're describing will get national recognition," Fredericks says, returning to his chair. "All right, you two. This kind of stunt will never happen again, do I make myself clear?"

Moments later, after you've fled the headmaster's office and are back in the crisp winter air, Walter pulls you into a hug. "You saved the day," he tells you. Relief courses through your veins—along with excitement at being so close to him again. That was way, way too close. Now all you have to do is produce the campaign, but that will be kind of amazing, too. And Hunter will get the help she needs. And you'll get to spend more time with Walter, which is the best part of all.

The End

SNAPSHOT #38

Sunday, February 16, 12:15 a.m.
Oberon

"Shall we call it a night?" Walter says gently.

"Sure!" you chirp, hoping you don't sound as desperate to go as you are. The situation with Walter has quickly grown beyond awkward. Ever since you turned away from his second kiss, the two of you have remained stuck on the dance floor, not meeting each other's eyes, trying to act as though nothing happened. It's just been a song or two, but it's felt like hours. Clearly, Walter's feeling pretty deflated. It's going to be a hell of a long plane ride back to Kings. You have no idea what to say to him—or even if you made the right decision in not letting things go any further.

Hunter is nowhere in sight. From a slightly less trafficked area near the front entrance, Walter tries to reach her on her cell, but after several attempts sends her a quick text instead. A moment later, he gets a response, and his brow furrows. "Huh. That's kind of strange," he says, mostly to himself.

"Is something wrong?"

"No, no. Hunter says the plane's waiting for us, she'll let the pilot know to take us home as soon as we show up."

"But?"

"It's just strange that she's holed up in some VIP room twenty feet away, and isn't bothering to come out and say goodbye to us in person. That's not the Helen I used to know." Seeing Walter hurt yet again—once by you, now by his beloved cousin—is more than you can handle. You reach out and touch his arm. He looks into your eyes briefly. "Anyway, we should go."

The two of you head for the door. There's a lump in your throat, and you can't help feeling like you've made a mistake you can't undo. Walter holds the door for you. Then he steps off the curb to hail a cab to take you back to Teeterboro Airport, which is outside of the city but still the nearest place for small planes to land. Not a cheap cab ride, by the way, but you're guessing he'll refuse to let you chip in for it. He's always been a perfect gentleman and a generous friend. Really, there's nobody you adore more than Walter. You think back on all the nights you've hung out in his room watching old movies. All the mundane Student Council meetings during which you'd passed notes back and forth to crack each other up. Should you just give it a chance? It's clear the dynamic between you has already been changed by that first kiss—what's the harm in seeing where the second one could take you?

And so, as the taxi whips through Manhattan, you lean across the backseat and kiss your best friend. It's even better the second time around. "I need to take this slowly," you tell him. "I don't know what I want yet, and I don't want to hurt you."

"I know," says Walter, who has clearly been launched to cloud nine. "No pressure. Just see how you feel." You curl up next to him and lay your head against his shoulder. It feels right—calm but exciting at the same time. The truth is, you can't imagine feeling better.

The End

SNAPSHOT #39

Sunday, February 16, 12:29 a.m.
Oberon

"Where are you going? Wait up!" Panic now courses through your veins. What did you just unleash by repeating that ladies' room rumor? Walter immediately charged off in search of his cousin. "You know you can't just confront her in the middle of a party, right?"

It's unclear whether he's heard you, given how fast he's moving through the packed club. You scurry after him to keep up. Finally, he spots the guy with a goatee to whom Hunter had been talking when you first arrived. "Have you seen my cousin?" he demands.

"Uh, probably the VIP room," Goatee Guy says, shrugging toward the back of the club before returning to the conversation he'd been having. Walter is off and running again toward a discreet black door.

"No dice," says the bouncer sitting outside of it.

"I'm Hunter Mathieson's cousin. Is she back there?"

"Sure you are. Sorry, buddy."

"Just tell me if she's in there!"

The bouncer stands—all three hundred pounds of him. "You're going to need to leave now," he tells Walter. His voice is low and steady, and yet this is not a gentle suggestion.

Walter's face is now so flushed with agitation that you're worried he could do something stupid—like pick a fight with the King Kong blocking your entrance. You step between him and the bouncer. "Could we just take a quick peek and see if she's in there?" you ask in your most polite, Kings Academy tour guide voice. The bouncer doesn't even bother to answer, making you feel pathetically young and powerless. You've felt out of your element since you arrived, but never more than now. You can't help but feel responsible for Walter's anguish, since you were the one to share the rumor. And what if it is just a baseless rumor? What if he's this worked up over nothing?

As much as this moment sucks, you're still grateful—strangely so—that Walter's no longer chatting it up with Carly the Magnificent. Instead, he's pleading with a man who could bench-press both of you at once without breaking a sweat. "Ask again and you're both on the street," the bouncer barks. Walter hangs his head but his feet don't move.

"Hey, Sal," says Carly, sweeping up behind you to kiss the bouncer on both cheeks. To your shock, Sal actually *smiles* at her. "Are you being mean? These are my friends. Walter here is Hunter's cousin."

"Had no idea they were with you, darling." There's not a flicker of hesitation as Sal swings open the door to let the three of you inside. Walter profusely thanks Carly, making you want to dissolve into the floor.

The VIP room feels anything but fabulous, in your opinion. Ominous and scary would be a more apt description. It's even darker than the rest of the club, a Goth cave with deep red velvet walls and black leather banquettes. It takes a second to spot Hunter, but the second you do, your worst fears are confirmed. She and her friends—who strike you immediately as the worst kind of night crawlers—are tucked into a nearby banquette, traces of white powder visible on the table in front of them. One of her group snorts a line, breaking Walter's freeze.

"We need to talk," he says to his cousin once he's in front of the table. "Now." You can't help feeling a bit impressed by how authoritative and strong he sounds. Carly looks at him with admiration, too. Hunter sputters for a moment, perhaps trying to formulate a defense, but she gets up and follows him. You and Carly stand apart as Walter takes on his cousin in the corner.

"He's a pretty amazing guy," Carly says. "You guys are close friends?"

You know exactly what she's asking. "Extremely," you tell her, hoping she'll take the cue and back off. Not likely, though. Carly seems to have immediately noticed what it took you months to see—that Walter is a major catch.

The two of you look over to the corner. Hunter nods her weak assent, and Walter takes her arm and leads her outside, through the club, toward the street. You and Carly follow without a word. You catch a view of Hunter's face, the shame in her eyes as evident as the heartbreak in Walter's.

Will Walter be able to help his cousin? Continue to Snapshot #39A (page 193) to find out.

SNAPSHOT #39A

Wednesday, June 4, 10:00 a.m.
The Quad

The campus, now fully thawed, is bursting with life and bare skin. Students have taken over the lush Quad, spreading out on blankets, sunbathing, playing Frisbee, pretending to read while scoping out the parade going by them. Somebody rigged speakers out on the roof of Pennyworth and now Bob Marley blasts through the honeysuckled air.

So much has changed since that Midwinter's Night.

Walter, for starters. Not only did Carly make him a campus legend when she came to visit for the first time, but she's also transformed him into a bona fide hottie—subtly changing both his hair and wardrobe over the past months. Word is out that Hunter is his cousin, too—launching him into the social stratosphere at Kings, not that he much cares.

You're happy for him, but there's no question that his romance with Carly has driven a wedge in your friendship. Your unexpected jealousy when she came onto the scene revealed your true feelings for Walter. But it was too little, too late—and now with Carly around, you don't get to see him as much.

Hunter, at Walter's insistence, has been regrouping at home with her parents after a full ninety days of rehab. Thankfully her drug issue has stayed under the media radar, allowing her to get stronger every day without any intrusion from the paparazzi. She's taking some more time off from work, Walter has told you, and is considering changes to her management team. And now that her parents understand the pressure she'd been under, they've gotten much more involved in her life. You're glad you didn't sit on that rumor.

That's not all that was set in motion on that frigid February night.

When you'd tiptoed into your dorm room at three in the morning, you were dismayed to find a tear-streaked Annabel sitting between Libby and Spider on the couch. To your shock, she and Henry were officially over. Apparently he'd said he wanted to see other people and she'd reluctantly let him go. But three months later, Henry is still fully single. You'd have heard if he'd paired up with anybody. He was as chaste as . . . well, as you. Out of loyalty to Annabel, you haven't spoken to Henry much since their breakup, other than your work together at the newspaper. But from time to time, you catch him looking at you during staff meetings in a way that—well, if it weren't such a crazy thought, you'd almost think Henry was interested in you. And a few times he's seemed to be on the verge of saying something before changing his mind and bringing up some random newspaper-related topic.

"Hopefully Worth will just give us our exam grades and let us go," Libby says as you walk together toward the history building. "I mean, what's the point of sitting through one more class? It's not like we're going to be tested on the stuff anymore."

Today is the last day of classes. Goodbye, freshman year. Your dad will be here tomorrow to load up the wagon and bring you home to Hope Falls, where a mellow summer of reading in the backyard hammock and working at a local camp awaits you. You've never been more excited to be in your hometown. Freshman year has been great, in so many ways, but you're in desperate need of a recharge.

"Hey, guys!" Walter calls, jogging to catch up with you.

"Hey, Wal!" Libby answers brightly. You're always happy to see him, but it's funny to see how Libby now lights up in his presence, too. You remember how she used to groan every time he showed up in your room.

"Are you all packed up?" you ask.

"Pretty much. I'm glad I got to see you. I was worried you might leave before we said goodbye."

"Walter, I would never do that! You know I would've come to find you tomorrow. Besides, my dad wants to see you."

"To rub in the Red Sox' record this season, no doubt." Walter laughs. "Listen, I was wondering if you'd ever want to come spend some time in Martha's Vineyard this summer. Maybe in August, when your camp is over? I know my folks would love to have you." He looks strangely shy, asking you this. "This spring has been so busy, I feel like you and I haven't had our usual time together. Would be nice to catch up."

You can't think of anything nicer, and you tell him so.

Maybe he does have room in his life for Carly and his friendship with you, after all. You stroll across the green, so exquisite it could be out of one of Hunter's big-budget movies. The summer ahead just got even better.

The End

SNAPSHOT #40

Sunday, February 16, 11:05 a.m.
Hamilton Dining Hall

"Why so glum?" asks Annabel after you've plopped down at a dining hall table with a stack of banana pancakes, hands down the best thing the cafeteria has to offer. If only you felt like eating. "Trust me, your night partying with Hollywood megastars sounds way more fabulous and memorable than last night's party. To tell you the truth, it was kind of awful. Libby got really drunk and Oona ended up crowning her the Freshman Mess, and all these guys doused her with beer. Spider and I had to lug her home, and the poor girl was shivering with cold. She'll be sleeping it off all day, I bet."

You poke at your pancakes, still not sure how to tell your friends that it's not missing out on last night's party that has you down. It's the memory of Walter and Carly's flirt-fest. Clearly, they were into each other—you'd practically had to pry Walter away from the leggy model with a crowbar so you didn't leave the plane waiting too long. Already they had plans to see each other again. You know you should be happy that your friend has landed such a trophy girl—but you're not. At all.

And your conscience is bugging you, too. True, you merely overheard a rumor about Hunter's drug use—but shouldn't you still pass that information along to Walter? If the rumor is true, it could really affect his cousin's health and well-being. He'd want to know.

"Spill," Spider commands. "Why do you look like you want to drown those pancakes in tears?"

And suddenly you're telling Spider and Annabel everything that's on your mind—your possible romantic feelings for Walter, your concern for Hunter, your worry that you may have just let a great guy slip between your fingers because you didn't appreciate just how right for you he really was. They just listen, taking it all in, and then, when you're all talked out, Annabel grabs your coat off the back of your chair and hands it to you.

"What are you waiting for?" she asks.

Spider pushes your card key and phone into your hand. "Trust me, if Walter knows you like him, it'll be 'Carly who?' You've got to go talk to him."

Are they right? And are you ready to take that plunge?

Eight nervous minutes later, you find yourself raising a fist to knock on Walter's door, half hoping he isn't home. What will you say if he is? Will you beg him to forget about the *Vogue*-worthy hottie who threw herself at him last night, and give you another chance?

Walter answers quickly, his hair wet from the shower. In comfy sweats and an old flannel shirt—not his usual

Wal-iform—he looks relaxed and really cute. As usual, he's got a coffee cup in one hand. Walter may be the one person who consumes more coffee than you. But he imports some über-gourmet beans for his morning joe, whereas you down the dining hall crap without thinking twice.

"Everything okay?" he asks, taking in the look on your face.

Words. Sentences. These would come in handy right about now. "Um, can I come in for a sec?" you ask.

"Of course! Coffee? I just made a pot."

"Thanks." You sit down on his couch, a tweedy hand-me-down from his parents, and try to think of the right entry ramp into this chat.

"Listen, I think I owe you an apology for last night," Walter says. "I hope I didn't make you uncomfortable."

You clear your throat. "Actually, Walter, I *was* uncomfortable. I wanted to be happy that you met this gorgeous girl who seems to have so much in common with you. But seeing you with Carly made me . . . well, jealous." You've never felt more vulnerable in your life, but at least it's out there. Even if you're flat-out rejected—which seems likely, given the competition—you gave it a shot.

Walter's face gives nothing away. "What are you saying? You were jealous because you think of me as more than a friend?" He sits on the coffee table across from you. It's a struggle to meet his eyes. It's crazy how fully these new feelings for Walter have rushed to the surface—or have you always felt this way?

"Um, yeah. Yes. I think I do." Your heart is thumping. He must be able to hear it.

The next thing you know, Walter leans forward and kisses you. And it's perfect. You feel a wave of relief, followed by one of enormous happiness. It's one of those magical moments when everything seems to fall into place. "You know I'm crazy about you," Walter tells you softly, making you melt even more. "I always have been. I was losing hope that you might ever feel the same way."

You lean over and kiss him again on the lips. It's surreal, but in the best way. You feel so transported that a few more yummy moments pass before you remember Hunter.

"There's something else I wanted to tell you," you say once you've pulled back from him a little. "Maybe it's nothing. It's just gossip I overheard in the ladies' room last night, so please take it with a tablet of salt, but it's been weighing on my mind. These girls insinuated that Hunter might have a drug problem. They didn't know her. Still, I thought you should know."

To your surprise, Walter just nods. "There was something weird going on last night. She disappeared into that back room and didn't bother coming out when I texted that we were leaving. She just texted me back a goodbye. I was no more than twenty feet away from her. That's completely unlike Helen. I'm going to get to the bottom of whatever's going on with her. Anyway, thank you. For telling me. I've already spoken to her parents and we're trying to figure out the best way to confront her."

You feel so relieved. Whether there's really an issue or not, Hunter is in good hands if Walter's on the case. It makes you feel even surer that you've made the right decision, coming to his door, opening yourself up to the prospect of romance with your friend.

"Where were we?" he asks, pulling you back into his arms.

With any luck, you're at the beginning of something really special.

The End

SNAPSHOT #41

Friday, March 21, 7:15 p.m.
Pennyworth House

"You guys are ridiculously cute," says Annabel as she pins your hair back into a loose knot at the nape of your neck. "And I have to say, I'm seeing a whole new side of Walter. He's so funny! I practically wet my pants laughing when he told us about getting attacked by ducks in Central Park."

You nod a little, trying not to move as the bobby pin goes in. Last night you and Walter—your boyfriend of over a month, crazy as that still sometimes seems—had finally had your first double date with Annabel and Henry at the local pizza place. She'd been begging you for weeks—well, ever since she'd barged in on you and Walter in a lip-lock with *Casablanca* playing in the background, Ingrid Bergman boarding her plane.

So here's the thing with Walter. Yes, you still occasionally cringe at the sight of that maroon sweater. Yes, you wish he wasn't so widely regarded as, well, a nerd. You know Libby is astounded that you'd hook up with someone with so little social currency. But on Midwinter's Night, you'd discovered that you have serious romantic chemistry with your best guy pal. It had come as a shock—but now, you can't imagine how you'd missed the great relationship that had been in front of you all along. You adore spending time with Walter, have a million things in common, and can't stop thinking about the next time you'll get to kiss him. So what if he's not Mr. Popular? Does it really matter? Your close friends have embraced him as one of the gang. Annabel jumped on board immediately, and so did Spider—and they seem to have instructed Libby to play nice or else. Now Walter is welcome to hang anytime.

Speaking of Spider—unfortunately, your suspicions about those final exams turned out to be true. The next morning at breakfast, your roommate had immediately confessed, tears in her eyes. Spider told you how much pressure she'd felt to pull up her grade in pre-calc . . . so much so that she'd gone against her better judgment and accepted some "illegal" help from some upperclassmen on her team. Worse, she thinks Oona knows her secret—explaining her stronger-than-average aversion to the girl. You convinced her to immediately shred the old exams—she hadn't needed much convincing—and you and Walter have been steadily tutoring her since. Every test is still a nail-biter, but she's doing fine now. Hopefully, Oona will keep her mouth shut.

The Queen of Mean has seemed uncharacteristically withdrawn since Mr. Worth stomped on her heart. You've spotted her walking to class in an oversize hoodie, her hair scraped back in a messy ponytail—this, from a girl who had her hair-dresser flown in weekly for a blowout and never showed up anywhere in less than a full-scale designer outfit. She clearly has other stuff on her mind besides Spider's transgressions. You can't help but feel sorry for Oona—and a little guilty about the fact that you didn't step in to comfort her when you had a chance.

When the bookstore in town burned to the ground on Midwinter's Night—the same night you'd witnessed Worth tell Oona the name of the other woman, Heather McPherson, who also happened to own the aforementioned bookstore—you'd immediately jumped to the worst conclusion about Oona. Thankfully, before you could go to the police accusing your schoolmate of arson, Heather came forward to admit to inad-vertently causing the fire herself. Apparently she'd been read-ing by candlelight and forgotten to blow out the flame before locking up. It struck you as a little odd, given how conscientious she'd always seemed to be—but accidents happened. Accord-ing to the local newspaper, Heather and her mother had since moved to a beautiful waterfront cottage in South Carolina, where she'd immediately opened a new shop. How she was able to afford it all was a mystery, even to the local reporter covering the story, since she hadn't been able to claim any money from insurance on her New Hampshire store. But in any case, she was apparently happy and thriving. You just miss the bookstore and her great recommendations.

There's a knock at the door, and Libby rushes to answer it. Tonight's the Spring Fling, and you've all been primping

—even Spider, who's going with Dexter Trent, a cute guy from her soccer team. Judging by Spider's state of nervous excitement, it's clear that she's very into him . . . and not other girls, as you'd once speculated with Annabel.

It's Henry at the door, looking dashing in a navy blue blazer and slightly too long chinos. As always, he exudes effortless cool and there's a little edge to his preppy style. He and Annabel got back together the week after their Midwinter's tiff. You've never been clear on the details of their reconciliation, but they seem pretty happy. She jumps up to greet him, but as they kiss at the door, you can't help but sense that he's aware of your presence in the room. Is that crazy? Just like last night, at pizza, when he kept . . . well, staring at you. Even when you weren't the one talking, Henry's eyes had seemed to linger on your face. Come to think of it, his behavior toward Walter was a bit strange, too. Henry was usually so warm and nice, and not one to care about whether someone was popular or not—but he'd been noticeably aloof with Walter. At times, he'd been borderline rude. When Walter was halfway through the duck story that had you and Annabel in stitches, Henry had excused himself to use the bathroom.

"You look beautiful," Henry says to Annabel, and she smiles. In her strapless black cocktail dress and mile-high Manolos, she's a vision of chic perfection. You're pleased with how your look turned out tonight, too. On your last weekend at home, you'd tried on the vintage shift dress in your mom's closet—a swirling kaleidoscope of color, with gold threads laced through like rays of sunlight. She wore it to prom with your dad and has saved it for you ever since. With her permission, you'd had it tailored to fit you just right. It looks pretty amazing with a pair of Annabel's platforms and a thick gold bangle.

Libby's date—a junior guy she knows from New York City, just a friend—arrives next with some blush-colored roses. She looks like a rose herself in shades of pink, her dress cinched at the waist and poufy. Gorgeous.

But it's Spider who will really cause the most jaws to drop. You and Annabel helped her find a beautiful pearlescent gray dress at the local mall. It's sweet, simple, and not too over-the-top girly—just right with her pretty curls loose on her shoulders. Spider has been so focused on school for the past few months—she'd confided that her GPA needed to come up or she'd lose her scholarship, so you've been spending a lot of time with her at Therot Library. Her hard work seems to be paying off, and she really deserves to have fun tonight.

Walter is the last to arrive, and when he does, you almost can't believe your eyes. He, like Spider, has been transformed. In a well-fitted suit and button-down, with his wild curls cut and tamed, he looks beyond cute . . . he looks hot! "Wow" is all you can say when you greet him.

Walter grins sheepishly, looking instantly more like himself. "My cousin had some pointers." He notices Libby gaping at him in disbelief and laughs. "No big deal."

"You mean Hunter?" Libby asks. The whole campus has been buzzing with the news that Walter has a megawatt famous relative. Apparently his cousin Helen, who'd spontaneously dropped by campus on Midwinter's Night but flown off to New York before you'd arrived at the diner, was actually Hunter Mathieson, the super-famous star last seen smooching Ashton Kutcher on the big screen. Walter and Hunter had been spotted walking together to Glory Days, ratcheting up his status among the cool crowd at Kings. Not that he cared. Frankly, you don't care much either. You love Walter for who he is—and what other people think has stopped being such a big deal.

After taking some pictures—several of which you immediately e-mail home to your mom—your group heads out for the dance, chattering happily. You slip your hand into Walter's and he lifts it to his lips to kiss it, sending a wave of bliss through your body.

Life is good. You've got the best friends, a guy you adore, and three more awesome years at Kings to look forward to. Tonight, in the deliciously warm spring air, you'll rock out with your crew under a beautiful white tent and have the time of your life. A great night lies ahead—with many more to follow.

The End

Saturday, February 15, 10:02 p.m.
Pennyworth House

"Hold on a second," you tell your friend, choosing each word carefully. You can't deny you felt something, but Walter means too much to you to just plunge into romance—and risk losing his friendship. "This feels really sudden. Can you give me some time to think about it? I just don't want to blow what we have."

Walter sits back, nodding. "Of course. No pressure. I'll always want to be friends, no matter what. I just hope there can be something more between us."

His response is so honest, so direct . . . so unlike your typical fifteen-year-old guy. Even though you've never really thought of Walter as a romantic prospect, you adore him so much that you're going to have to open your mind to the possibility. But as long as he doesn't mind being a bit patient, there's no reason to rush.

The door to Pennyworth 304 swings open, and both of your heads turn to see Annabel stumble inside. At first you think she must be drunk—she can barely control the path of her long limbs, and she bumps into the corner of Libby's dresser with her hip. "Damn," she scowls, rubbing it hard.

"You okay?" you ask her.

"No," she says. "I'm not." She's not drunk, you realize, taking in her tear-streaked cheeks and red eyes. She's heartbroken.

"I'll leave you guys alone," Walter says, quickly excusing himself from the room.

Annabel sinks into his spot on the couch and pulls her knees up to her chest. There are twigs and leaves caught in her long dark hair. "Henry and I broke up," she says, hugging her shins and suddenly choking back a fresh round of tears.

It's like the air's been vacuumed out of the room. She can't be serious. They're the perfect couple! You're so stunned you can barely get out a response. "Did you have a fight or something? Whatever it is, I'm sure you can work it out."

Annabel shakes her head almost violently from side to side. "No, no, no. It's over. He doesn't"—another gut-wrenching sob—"love me. He wants to see other people."

That's even more bizarre. Who could hold a candle to your beautiful, smart, kind, funny best friend? She is literally as good as it gets. "I'm so sorry, Annabel. I don't even know what to say." You give her a hug, and she goes limp in your arms. Then she pulls back to wipe her nose with a soggy-looking tissue.

"Were you and Walter watching *Casablanca*?" It's an abrupt subject change, but clearly Annabel's trying to distract herself. You follow her lead.

"For the millionth time. He's even more obsessed than I am." You point to the Scrabble game, where Walter's I ♡ U stretches across the whole board like a blaring headline. "We had an interesting night. I think there may be something there, but I'm just not sure."

"With Walter?"

"I know. Weird, right?"

Annabel looks at you closely, her eyes rimmed in red. "It's not weird. I mean, I've always known he had a thing for you. And he's a really good guy. Solid. Loyal. Not the type to callously throw you aside the way Henry just did to me." Whoa. You have a feeling that Henry-bashing might be the new sport around your room for quite a while. "Do you think you're going to give him a chance?"

Before you can answer, Spider crashes through the door. "Holy crap!" she pants, racing to the window and pulling back the curtains. "Did you guys hear the sirens earlier? I just got a text from a girl on my team. Apparently the bookstore in town burned down!" You and Annabel rush over to see, and sure enough, there's smoke coming from the direction of town. Holy shit. Oona. Could she have done this? Was she so incensed by Worth's rejection that she'd commit arson, burning down Heather's store in a fit of rage? Before you know it, you're telling Annabel and Spider exactly what you saw. The words spill out before you even consider what you're saying.

"You think Oona burned the lady's store down?" Annabel looks back at the fire incredulously. "I know she's crazy, but is she *arson* crazy?" The three of you just stare at each other, nobody sure of the answer.

"It could be a coincidence," you say, glancing back at the funnel of smoke rising up from the town.

"Just be careful," Spider says. "You don't want Oona as an enemy."

"And accusing a fellow schoolmate of a felony is no small thing," Annabel adds.

"Honestly, guys, I have no idea what to do," you say. "Just keep it between us for now."

"Hellllllloooo!" Libby breaks the moment, coming home with her face flushed from a night of serious boozing. The three of you try to act normal, and fortunately Libby's mind is fully elsewhere. "Did you hear that Hunter Mathieson was on campus tonight? Apparently someone saw her walking with *Walter* to Glory Days!" Gossip this major has Libby's eyes bulging with glee.

"That's ridiculous." You laugh. "He was with his cousin Helen earlier."

But hang on a second.

Is it possible that Hunter Mathieson is aka Walter's cousin Helen, who left Glory Days to head back to New York just minutes before you arrived to meet him there? Hunter Mathieson, international megastar, last seen on the big screen locking lips with Ashton Kutcher? Suddenly, you can kind of see it—they share the same great bone structure, they both have eyes that are shockingly blue. And it'd be so like Walter to not even think to mention that Helen—that bullfrog-catching cousin with whom he shared many a happy camping trip as a kid—just commanded twenty million bucks for an upcoming chick flick in which she plays Julia Roberts's wayward daughter.

"Call him right this second!" Libby practically yells, shoving the phone in your face. Maybe it's immature, but you're thrilled. Libby's reaction will be universal. If Hunter really is his cousin, Walter will be the guy everyone wants to know. No matter what happens between the two of you, life at Kings will be easier for him if he's considered somewhat cool. And having such a famous relative pretty much locks that in.

"I promise I'll call him first thing tomorrow." You look over at Annabel, who looks like she might collapse to the floor from emotional exhaustion. "I think we all need to call it a night." Frankly, you're dying to be horizontal, too—maybe then you can sort out what you should do next about Walter and Oona. And then there's the conversation you'll need to have with Spider about those tests you found. And last, your head can't help swirling a little with thoughts of Henry, now single. He just devastated your best friend, and you know it's awful to feel this way, but it seems impossible to shut down your attraction to the guy.

Annabel falls into her bed, and you go to pull down the window shade. "Could we leave it open tonight?" she asks, and you nod, padding up the ladder to your top bunk.

Annabel turns off the light, and the two of you lie watching the flakes of snow petal down outside the window, softly lit by a streetlamp below. You try not to think about the distant smoke, no longer visible from your bedroom, and what it means for poor Heather McPherson.

The End

ABOUT THE AUTHOR

Bridie Clark has worked as a book and magazine editor. Her novels *Because She Can* and *The Overnight Socialite* have been published in nineteen countries.